THE
RAVENOUS
GOWN

D1308196

Your best
fairy tale of all – may you
live it happily, ever-after.

PRAISE FOR STEFFANI RAFF AND *THE RAVENOUS GOWN*

"These stories will inoculate girls against the full force of the idea that you have to fit society's idea of beauty in order to be loved. This book is about being yourself, about claiming your goodness, smartness, and your inherent attractiveness regardless of the exact shape of your nose. The stories in this book are delightful, they are wonderful art, and together, they paint a picture of a reality we are hungry for but it is so hard to get a clear picture of."

—DOUG LIPMAN, internationally known, award-winning author of *Improving Your Storytelling*

"*The Ravenous Gown* is filled with powerful stories of beauty and strength. With dragons, princes, curses and princesses (who are more than their beautiful gowns), the stories transported me to enchanting worlds and left me wanting more. Steffani Raff is a wordsmith who has created something beautiful, by all definitions of the word."

—PAIGE FUNK, blogger at *Intellectual Recreation*

"Steffani Raff is a talented storyteller. Her amazing stories remind us that love conquers all, fear can be overcome, and everyone has a hero inside."

—ELIOT WILCOX, Executive Director of the Timpanogos Storytelling Institute

Familius books are available at special discounts for bulk purchases for sales promotions, family, or corporate use. Special editions, including personalized covers, excerpts of existing books, or books with corporate logos, can be created in large quantities for special needs. For more information, contact Premium Sales at 559-876-2170 or email specialmarkets@familius.com

Library of Congress Catalog-in-Publication Data
2014959240

Paperback ISBN 978-1-939629-59-3
Hardcover ISBN 978-1-942672-75-3
Ebook ISBN 978-1-942672-02-9

Printed in the United States of America

Edited by Lindsay Sandberg
Cover Design by David Miles
Book Design by Brooke Jorden

10 9 8 7 6 5 4 3 2 1
First Edition

This book is dedicated to my daughters,
Abby and EmmyLou.

ACKNOWLEDGMENTS

I would like to express heartfelt thanks and sincere appreciation to all those who believed in and encouraged me to write *The Ravenous Gown*.

The team at Familius has championed this book from the beginning. Thank you especially to my editor, Lindsay, and David, whose encouragement kept me writing.

Thank you to the many people who read or listened to these stories and offered valuable feedback to help this book become what it is today. My daughter, Abby Raff; her friends Kaylee, Katie, and Brianna, and her high school English teacher, Mrs. Childs; Regi Carpenter; Mariah Fralick and her daughters; Paige Funk; Randy and Brittney Henderson, and their children; Joanne Hall; Karla Huntsman; Erika Nelson; Ginger Parkinson; ToriAnn Perkey; Joey Raff; Wendy Rupper, and her daughter, Cheri Schulzke; Heleen Wittusen; and the Timp Tellers chapter of the Utah Storytelling Guild.

Much more than mere thanks goes to Doug Lipman whose generous gift of time, talent, and attention not only helped shape the stories in this book, but the woman who wrote them.

And finally, my husband, Kevin; without him there would be no book. Thank you, Kevin, for not only encouraging me, but for making space and time for me to create. Thank you for using your skills and talents to support me. And thank you for seeing and believing in my real beauty before I could. I am forever blessed to have you for my husband.

CONTENTS

THE RAVENOUS GOWN

Once upon a time, there was a princess who found herself in the scullery, peeling potatoes.

"I don't think this is what my parents had in mind when they sent me to prevent a war," the Princess muttered to herself as she paced the kitchen. "It's obvious I can't do anything dressed like this." She twirled in her blackened gown, and tiny bits of ash fell to the floor, strands of frizzled hair stood on end and flopped into her face, and the dusky smell of smoke filled the air. The Princess slumped onto a stool, picked up a potato, and lopped off a chunk.

"It would take a fairy godmother to get me out of this mess," the Princess said with a simpering smile. As soon as the words spilled out of her mouth, POOF, her fairy godmother appeared.

"What?" The Princess waved away the colored sparkles hanging in the air. "Who are you?"

"I am your fairy godmother."

"Really?"

The tiny, glowing figure smiled. "Really."

"I didn't think you actually existed. I thought you were just some convenient literary device used in fairy tales to grant wishes to deserving princesses who found themselves in need."

"That is exactly what I do, my dear."

"Really? Well, if that is case, I could really use a wish right now."

"What is it?"

"I wish to look like I did before my unfortunate mishap with the dragon."

"A dragon? Oh, my dear, what happened?"

"I was nestled inside my kingdom's finest carriage, enjoying my breakfast, when a dragon pounced on my entourage.

"The knights were gallant and fended off the dragon for as long as they could, but, in the end, their swords were no match for flames.

"From what I could see out the window, it looked like it was just me and the dragon. Luckily, I had just finished my studies on the history and sociology of dragons. I knew that dragons were not touted for being patient creatures, especially when it comes to food. I also knew that dragons never refuse a challenge.

"I could hear the dragon's nostrils sniffing outside the carriage, so I grabbed the last hard-boiled egg from my breakfast and opened the carriage door. I shouted, 'I challenge you to a—'

"But before I could finish, the dragon hiccupped, and a tiny burst of flame hit me and singed me from head to toe.

"I waved the smoke away, cleared my throat, and finished, 'I challenge you to a duel of strength. If I win, you let me and anyone left of my company go free. If you win, you decide our fate.'

"The dragon's smile was hideous. Blood-red gums and scores of sharp teeth. The dragon hissed, 'I accept your challenge. I enjoy playing with my food.'"

The fairy godmother gasped, "Oh, how awful!"

"I was terrified, but I couldn't very well let the dragon know that. I stooped to the ground and picked up what looked like two small stones, but only one was a stone. The other was that hard-boiled egg from my breakfast. I gulped down fear, then looked at the dragon and said, 'I have two small stones in my hands. Whoever can crush the stone with their bare hands first, wins the challenge.'

"The dragon opened his long, clawed hand. I climbed into it and gave him the stone. I climbed back down and yelled, 'Let us begin!' The dragon closed his fist tight, but the stone was so small it lodged between two of his scales.

"The dragon opened his fist and tried to pry out the stone using his terrible claws, which, incidentally, were terrible for dislodging small objects from scales. The dragon roared, and his flame burned down my carriage.

He swished and banged his tail on the ground, sending great plumes of dirt in the air. He made an awful ruckus.

"I waited for the dragon's little tantrum to end, and, when I was sure I had his full attention, I held my arm up and squeezed the egg in my hand. It made a satisfying CRACK, then squished inside my fist. I looked the dragon in the eye and smiled.

"The dragon bellowed.

"And I bellowed back, 'We had a deal. Now go!'

"The dragon snapped his teeth, whipped his body around, and took flight. I almost collapsed, but knew I had to get to the banquet. My parents were counting on me to soothe tensions between our kingdoms, so I walked the rest of the way to the castle.

"I didn't bother cleaning myself up; surely, the King, Queen, and Prince would understand when I told them what happened . . . but I never got the chance."

"What? Why not?" The fairy godmother's tiny face had an expression of perfect outrage.

"When I finally convinced the guard to let me enter and rushed into the great hall to tell them why I was late, the King took one look at me and told his servants to throw me back into the scullery where I belonged!"

"No!"

"Yes!" A small chuckle escaped the Princess at this farcical predicament. "And that is why I am *attempting* to peel potatoes." The Princess smiled at her lopsided, partially peeled potato, then looked up at the fairy and said,

"And why I am in need of a wish."

"Tell me what you wish my dear, and I shall grant it." More sparkles filled the air as the fairy godmother took out her wand.

"I wish to look like I did this morning before I met that nasty dragon."

"Are you sure that is all you want? Opportunities like this don't come every day."

"Yes, I am sure. I think I can handle the situation from there. Thank you." The Princess was about to add *I am so glad you are real,* but it sounded so ridiculous in her mind she just smiled warmly instead.

POOF!

And there she was—dressed exactly as she had been before. The Princess wore a delicate, floor-length gown the first color of sunset, the color that says, "stop, slow down, something spectacular is about to happen." Her hair cascaded in perfect curls around her face and was intertwined with rose petals and pearls. She wore one-of-a-kind shoes made of fine white leather. From curls to shoes, the Princess was dazzling.

She walked into the dining room once again. This time, when she walked in, every person stopped to look at the Princess.

"Ah, Princess Isabella, you have finally arrived. Come and take your place as our esteemed guest of honor," the King proclaimed.

"Thank you, Your Majesty." The Princess curtsied.

"Servants, bring this lovely lady some food. She must be famished."

The servants lined up with great platters of food. The Princess smiled and accepted the bread and soft cheese from the first tray.

She broke the bread in half and jammed the two chunks into the sleeves of her dress. Then she smeared the soft cheese across the bodice. "Eat well, my pretty dress," she said, and flashed her daintiest smile.

The next servant offered meat, potatoes, and gravy.

The Princess took the meat right off the platter and stashed it in the sash around her middle. She took handfuls of potatoes and smashed them into the folds of fabric around her hips. The gravy she carefully drizzled over the entire skirt in a rather delicate pattern. "Eat well, my pretty dress."

The entire court now watched, waiting to see what she would do with the cake on the next platter. The servant lowered the cake and pulled out a knife to cut her a piece.

The King had stopped breathing. His face was red and splotchy. The Queen turned away. The Prince was so astonished by this Princess that he watched in wonder as she took the cake and filled her shoes with it. "Eat well, my pretty shoes," she smiled.

"What is the meaning of this?" the King boomed. "How dare you come to our table, late, and act like this! What do you have to say for yourself?" The King was sputtering in his rage.

The Princess stood and addressed them. "Earlier this evening, I came to the dining hall to take my place as the guest of honor . . . and I was thrown out. Why? Because my clothing was singed and blackened, my hair a mess, and my shoes in shambles due to an unfortunate mishap with a dragon.

"Luckily, my fairy godmother made a surprise appearance and gifted me with these clothes—the very clothes I would have come in had I not met up with that nasty dragon. When I arrived in these clothes, I was immediately offered a place at your table as an esteemed guest.

"That is when I understood it was not me you invited to the banquet at all. It was my clothing. And so it was my clothing that enjoyed the meal."

A lump of potatoes dropped to the floor. So did the Prince's chin; he was smitten.

A happy alliance between kingdoms was made after all.

THE MAGIC MIRROR

A long time ago in a kingdom far, far away, there lived a King who was as handsome as he was noble; as kind as he was rich; as wise as he was good. And he was single.

But finding a wife was challenging. In this kingdom, there were no easy arranged marriages with princesses from far distant shores. Instead, the King was required by custom to find a bride from within the kingdom.

He took his problem to his most trusted advisor: his barber.

"How will I ever find a bride?" the King sighed.

"You could throw a ball."

"A ball?" the King laughed. "I'd be so occupied with the next dance step, I'd hardly have time to think about who would make a wonderful companion." The King sighed again. "Marriage is like this stool. If the legs aren't equal, it won't hold any weight. That's what my father taught me and what his father taught him. Ruling a kingdom is a heavy weight, and I want someone who will bear it with me."

"It will be challenging to find a woman who is your equal; you are the King."

"I am the King, but I am also just a man, my friend. How do you see what is inside a woman?" The King ran his fingers through his hair. The barber ceased snipping momentarily.

The barber smiled, "I'm not sure how seeing a woman's insides is going to help—a rather messy affair, I'd think."

The King's laugh surged out slowly, like a bird hatching from an egg. "You are a good man."

The next day, the barber presented the King with a gift—a mirror nestled in a box lined with soft, dark fabric.

"Your Majesty, I offer this mirror as a gift to assist you in choosing a bride. The mirror is magical and will reflect a woman's flaws on its surface as a splotch. In your search for an equal, may it help you discern what the eyes cannot."

The King posted a proclamation inviting any eligible lady to come and view herself in his magical mirror. Any woman who could see herself without a splotch would be deemed a worthy bride, and the King would court her for his wife.

The King expected to see a great line of eligible ladies lined up at the castle gates, but there was not a woman in sight.

Not on this day, or the next, or the next . . . or the next.

For no matter how kind or lovely, willing or winsome, each woman was, each knew her own flaws.

The women went to great lengths to encourage their flawless friends to attempt a look in the magical mirror.

"You really should look in the King's magic mirror. You are perfect for him," a woman coaxed her friend.

"No, I'm not. The extra flub on my tummy will show up as a splotch!" she replied.

"At least you don't have freckles," said another woman.

"Or big toes," said another.

"I have too much flub on my backside."

"I wish I had any flub at all," another woman chimed in.

Dangling earlobes, big hands, guilty pleasures, snoring, impatience, bushy eyebrows, a tendency to be boring, bossiness, thin lips, a chatty disposition, clumsiness, and occasional crabbiness all kept women from looking in the King's mirror.

No woman wanted to see a splotch in her reflection, nor did she want anyone else to see her imperfections.

Months passed, and no one came to the castle to look in the mirror, until one spring day, a shepherd girl came into town for the annual shearing of her sheep. She spent so much time in the mountains she knew nothing of the King's magic mirror. She read the proclamation and approached the castle gate.

"I will look in the King's mirror," she said simply.

A great trumpeting went forth; a woman would actually approach the mirror. Women from all over the kingdom gathered to see who among them dared to view their own reflection.

"Who is she?"

"I don't know. I've never seen her."

"She must not come into town much."

"That is obvious. She is wearing such simple clothing."

"Look at how her skirt is hiked up to show her ankles."

"Her ankles! They are so large."

"Her hair is slipping out of that braid."

"She smells like sheep."

The women couldn't help themselves. Here was such an obviously flawed woman approaching the King's mirror.

The shepherdess stood listening to the whispers, waiting for the King.

When he saw her, the King smiled. He had waited for this day for almost a year.

"You are aware of the magical properties of this mirror?" the King asked in a hushed tone.

"Yes," she said simply.

"And you are willing to look at your own reflection, unafraid?"

"Yes," she said, then faced the crowd of women gathered.

"I know that I am not perfect, but according to the proclamation, the King isn't looking for perfection; he is looking for an equal. Even the King, as wonderful and wise as he is, is not perfect." She turned to the King. "No offense is meant by this, Your Majesty."

"None was taken," he smiled.

She addressed the crowd, "In appearance, you find me lacking, but clothing and features fade with time. I am happy with who I am today, and I am happy with who I will be tomorrow."

She looked at the mirror.

Not a single splotch appeared.

The silence broke when a woman from the crowd grabbed the mirror from the shepherdess to view her own face. Not a single splotch appeared. "What!?"

Woman after woman grabbed the mirror, horrified to view their own reflection—splotchless.

"The mirror must be broken!"

"This mirror isn't magical at all."

"It's a fake!"

The barber shared a sidelong glance with the King and shrugged with a grin. The King laughed, delighted with the discovery.

"It seems every woman in the kingdom is fit to be your bride," the barber smiled.

"It seems so, but I choose to court the only woman who was willing to look in the mirror and accept whatever she saw. That is, if she will allow me."

The shepherdess nodded her head and smiled.

The women continued to pass the mirror from person to person. Some saw themselves as beautiful for the first time, while others looked in the mirror, convinced it was broken. And they all lived as happily as they allowed themselves to be.

CINDERELLA—SORT OF

"Grandmamma, what happened to your foot?"

"How come you are missing part of your heel?"

"The answer to those questions, my loves, is a story," said the grandmother.

"Tell us the story," three eager grandchildren chimed. The boy with freckles sat at the foot of the rocking chair and placed his head on her lap. The girl with inquisitive eyes watched her grandmother from the floor. And the girl with a propensity for romantic ideas sat on the fireplace hearth to keep warm and have a view of her siblings' reactions to their grandmother's story.

"Well, children, there was a time when I thought living happily ever after meant one thing and one thing only: marry the Prince."

"Prince Henry?" said Inquisitive Eyes.

"He's only eleven!" said Romantic Ideas, stunned.

"Not Prince Henry," the grandmother laughed. "His grandfather, King Gerald. But he was only Prince Gerald back then."

"Oh," they all said in unison.

"A long time ago, when my hair was the color of raven feathers and my cheeks flushed the color of roses, I held in my hands a most unusual opportunity. Prince Gerald had signed and sealed an invitation to every eligible young lady in the kingdom to attend a ball. He was going to break a tradition that had been standing among royalty since time began. He would choose a bride from within the kingdom. A commoner! It was unheard of! A commoner marry a prince?!

"I had scarcely read the words of the proclamation before my mind was caught up in a dream.

"I was dancing with the Prince, wearing a gown the same green as my eyes. I was captivating. The swish of my dress, the gentle ring of our laughter, the joy in our eyes—it was true love. I would be a princess. And what a different life that would be: no long hours toiling over someone else's clothing, no worrying about how or where I would get enough to eat. I would have servants and privileges. I would have prominence and prosperity. And I would have a handsome husband.

"But it was only a dream. I didn't have a dress for the ball. And even though I had the talent to make a dress, I knew with an announcement like this, I would be working every lighted hour at the dress shop for Mrs. Fister. Every girl in the kingdom would order a new dress. I would be so busy sewing their dresses, I wouldn't have time to sew a gown of my own.

"Each night, I worked on dresses by candlelight. I worked until my fingers ached, until the fabric blurred in front of me. I hoped by working thus I would have enough time to sew something for myself. But the orders just kept coming in.

"The night before the ball, a devious plan took shape in my mind. One client could not decide on whether she wanted a red dress or a green dress, so she had the audacity to order both! The red dress was finished, and it was a wonder. The color was divine, and you should have seen the way the sash clung to her waist, then burst into a bow in the back. The dress was perfect.

"I was still working on the green dress. I could get it done if I worked all through the night—unless . . . "

"Unless what, Grandmamma?" asked Romantic Ideas.

A sweet, naughty smile slipped onto the grandmother's face. "Unless I altered it so it would fit me instead. She had two choices, after all. She would look dashing in the red gown, and I could wear the green gown.

"You didn't!" exclaimed Freckles.

"I did!" the grandmother laughed. "After everyone left the shop, I stayed under the pretense of finishing the dress. I held the green gown, soft and silky, in my hands for a very long time, and finally, all at once, I tried it on. I started pinning the needed alterations and customizations. I sewed and sewed, then tried the dress on again. It fit perfectly. I twirled in front of the mirror; I had transformed into the beautiful girl in my dreams. I was going to the ball. I would win the hand and heart of the Prince.

"But suddenly, I heard a crash at the front of the store. If anyone saw me, I would lose my employment and perhaps, much more.

"I dove behind some bolts of fabric, heart pounding, tears welling, body shaking. I held my breath and willed myself to listen.

"I heard a gentle scraping on the floor. A rattling by the door. Someone was there, and I was as good as caught."

The children were up on their knees, faces anxious in the warm, golden light of the room.

"What happened?" Freckles asked, unable to bear the suspense any longer.

"It was a cat!" The grandmother laughed.

"A cat?!"

"Yes, a cat! When I went home that night, I purposefully left an unfinished sleeve and hem on the dress. The next day the client was furious when I told her the green dress was not done.

"'Oh,' she said, 'this red dress is divine, but where is the green one?'

"'I worked all through the night but couldn't finish. I'm sorry,' I said.

"'This is unacceptable,' she screamed. 'I wanted both dresses!'

"'I'm sorry,' I said. 'I did what I could, but—'

"'Where is the head seamstress here? She will hear of my displeasure!' she continued ranting.

"That's when Mrs. Fister came in and got an earful about dresses and the cost of dresses and unfulfilled orders and unfulfilled expectations.

"That's when I got an earful about dress making and keeping clients happy and how the price of the dress would come out of my salary."

"But you didn't lose your job?" asked Inquisitive Eyes.

"No, I didn't," said the grandmother, then continued. "When the dresses were all collected, Mrs. Fister closed up the shop early. She had two daughters of her own to get ready for the ball. I stayed with the promise that I would finish the green dress and it would be ready for the client in the morning.

"I went right to work on the sleeve and the hem, and in no time, I had the dress on and my hair pinned up in a most elegant style. I pinched my cheeks, then looked in the mirror. It was the most beautiful I had ever looked. I was even more beautiful than I thought I could look. I would win the Prince's admiration—I was sure of it.

"With so many women and so many dresses, no one would realize the dress I wore was supposed to be for some else."

"Grandmamma, I can't believe you did that!" said Freckles.

"Yes, it's perfectly horrible!" said Inquisitive Eyes.

"It's perfectly wonderful, you mean!" said Romantic Ideas. "Tell us about the ball! What happened?"

"Fine, fine. On with the story. The ball. The ball was colorful. So many women, so many dresses, so many glowing eyes, so much anticipation. The smell of a thousand flowers in the air.

"There was a banquet of food, but no one dared eat. We all waited for the Prince.

"Then it was trumpets and uniforms and, finally, the Prince. Tall and slender in his finest royal attire. Tall boots. A brocade jacket. His wavy dark hair swooped across his face, and his dark eyes were smiling. He was even more handsome than I imagined!"

"He's old and fat now," said Freckles, giggling.

"Ho! Ho! True enough, but back then he wasn't," the grandmother replied smiling. "His eyes swept the room. Women put on their most charming smiles, even as they nudged and pushed each other out of the way for better position. Then his eyes stopped."

"On Cinderella?" asked Inquisitive Eyes.

"No," said the grandmother. "On me."

"What?" they all said in surprise.

"He strode the distance between us and asked me to dance. The music swelled and filled the hall as we danced. Just like I dreamed, except the Prince didn't say a word. He just held me in his strong arms and led me across the floor. When the music changed, he kissed my hand, thanked me, and in a few steps, he was gone, dancing with another beautiful woman dressed in a lilac-colored gown. I watched in wonder as the Prince switched women dance after dance and sometimes in between.

"Then I heard a voice close to my ear. 'Pardon me,' it said. 'May I have this dance?'

"'Yes,' I whispered. I turned around and took the hand of a royal guard. His uniform made him stiff on the dance floor, but he had me laughing in minutes. He mixed flattery with kind-hearted jabs at the banquet. I added a few jabs myself that brought such a smile to his face. I almost missed his smile, though, because I was so busy looking for the Prince. The dance floor was littered with so many couples now, it was difficult to see him.

"The Royal Guard and I visited the banquet tables, pretended to eat, and continued to laugh.

"I had to leave the ball early to make the alterations on the dress I was wearing, so it would be ready for the client the next morning. I dared not displease this particular customer again.

"I hoped to see a glimpse of the Prince before I left, but it was not to be.

"I danced around and around the dress shop in my underslip, recreating my moment with the Prince. I was filled with hope. After all, he chose to dance with me first.

"For several days, nothing happened. Then, I received a letter from the King. The Prince had fallen in love with a woman in the kingdom, but he did not know her name or how he could find her. My face flushed at the news—it could be me. A royal entourage would be visiting each house in the kingdom to try a glass slipper on the foot of every eligible maiden. If the shoe fit, she would be chosen as the Prince's bride. What would life be like? A real princess. No more sewing dresses, at least, not unless I felt like it. Nothing to worry my head over—just pure bliss.

"When the royal entourage arrived at my home, I slid the glass slipper on my foot with the careful patience of threading a needle. My toes fit the shoe perfectly; but there was a small chunk of my heel that wouldn't make its way into the shoe, even if I arched my foot. If I could just get this slipper to fit, my whole life would be different, better. My foot was entirely hidden by the underskirts of my dress, and in a moment of desperation, I slipped my sharp sewing scissors under my dress and snipped off part of my heel. I swallowed the stab of pain that clawed up my leg and smiled, 'It fits.'

"A great commotion began. 'We've found her! The shoe fits!' The Prince burst through the door with an elated smile, which deflated when he saw me. 'The shoe fits?' he said, confused.

"I swallowed, then beamed at him, 'Yes!' I minced the distance between us hoping he was true to his word, but he wasn't looking at me; he was looking at the floor. 'What is that?' he asked. I had left a trail of blood behind me. 'Show me your foot,' he commanded. I lifted my skirts to reveal a slipper sloshing with blood. I turned away, too afraid of what would happen next. The Prince touched my arm with such tenderness; I looked at his face. 'You were not the first to use such measures, nor will you be the last, but I cannot marry you,' he said.

"The royal party left in swift procession, carrying with them the shoe and my dreams of a better life. I was left sobbing on the floor with a bloody foot and no hope of repairing it.

"I wrapped my foot in cloth and hobbled into the dress shop—and when I walked in . . . he was there."

"The Prince?" gasped Romantic Ideas.

"No. The Royal Guard I had danced with. When he saw me, he swooped over to my aid. 'What happened?' he said, not trying to hide the alarm in his voice.

"'An accident,' I stammered.

"'You walked here with your foot like that?'

"'Yes,' I said bewildered.

"'This will never do,' he said. 'When do you go home at night?'

"'Just before sunset,' I replied.

"'I will be here to escort you home on my horse.'

"And that is how your grandpapa and I fell in love."

"Grandpapa was the Royal Guard?" Freckles asked in wonder.

"Yes," the grandmother smiled.

"Did you ever tell him the truth?" asked Romantic Ideas.

"Yes, she did," a deep voice interjected. They all jumped, surprised to see their grandfather standing behind their grandmother. He continued the story. "Several years after we were married, she came to me with her little confession. She told me the story of how much she wanted to be a princess. To have that life. So much, in fact, she was willing to snip off part of her foot to do it."

"Then I told him how happy I was to be married to him instead," said the grandmother.

"And I replied, 'But I'm no prince.'"

"And I told him, 'You don't have to be a prince to be charming. Besides, I'm no Cinderella.'"

"That's when I swept your grandmamma up in my arms and said, 'You never had to be.' Then we kissed like this," said the grandfather, kissing his wife.

"Are you done yet?" Freckle's voice interjected itself into this *happily ever after*.

"Done with what?" the grandparents asked in mock innocence.

"Kissing!" said Inquisitive Eyes, horrified.

"Grandparents don't kiss," Romantic Ideas chimed in.

"Especially not in front of grandchildren," said Freckles.

"But it wouldn't be happily ever after without a kiss!" Grandmother laughed and kissed her husband again.

THE LOST PRINCESS

It was the celebration of the century.

She came, though uninvited, ate a cream puff, and cursed the child.

"The Princess will appear to be whatever people think of her." The malevolent fairy faced the court and royal family, and with a bold and fluid movement, curtsied, then disappeared.

The King chuckled, drawing the silent eyes of those assembled to him. "Silly fairy." He tossed the words out in unconcerned scorn and spoke again with confidence. "The entire kingdom loves—no adores, Princess Ronwynn. She will continue to look exactly as she is, a beloved and beautiful princess. There is absolutely no need to worry about a curse like that. It has no power here."

The Princess gurgled in happy tones, the King called for music, and the celebration resumed.

When both music and light were extinguished from

the castle, the fairy crept through it, sprinkling magic dust on every soul. When she reached the royal family's chamber, she blew the remaining dust into the faces of the King and Queen and smirked. "Silly fairy? We shall see." And the fairy scooped the Princess right out of the Queen's arms. When the castle awoke three days later, it was too late; the Princess was gone.

The fairy took the tiny Princess just beyond the warmth of the kingdom to a dirty hovel at the edge of the woods. She removed the Princess's fine nightgown and wrapped her tight in a stinking cloth. She rubbed the baby's rosy cheeks and fine blonde hair with ash and dirt, then abandoned her outside the hovel's door.

The Princess cried and the door opened. Standing at the door was a woman with a sneer on her face, matted hair, and sunken eyes.

"What is this?" she croaked like a frog. "I hope it's something I can eat for breakfast." She picked the child up and held her close to her face. Her eyes widened, and she almost dropped the bundle. "This is a child! I can't eat that!"

The Princess reached out with her chubby arm to touch the woman's nose. The woman let out an exasperated sigh. "Where did you come from?" The Princess was too young to know or answer. The woman sneered, "You look like a dirty little rat." Then the woman smiled. "But rats, no matter how dirty, are smart and can be trained. You may prove yourself useful yet." The woman's piggy eyes gleamed at the thought of someone to do her chores. "You will be *my* dirty rat, won't you?" the woman crooned.

The Princess cooed in response. Her fine, blonde hair began the subtle transformation to coarse and greyish-brown, like rat fur.

The curse would be a problem here.

The woman fed and clothed the Princess. She taught her how to gather sticks for kindling, how to tell which berries and mushrooms were edible, and how to cook a pot of mush.

"Where's my dirty little rat? I need some wood for the fire," the woman would call.

"I am here," said the Princess.

"What are you, my pet?"

"I am a dirty rat." The Princess's response was always the same.

"That's right. Now, show me what a useful little rat you are, and fetch me some wood." The woman smiled.

The curse worked its magic on the Princess's features. Her chin now sloped into her neck, her upper teeth protruded outward, along with her nose. Her hair looked mangy, ragged, and coarse. Her back was stooped and rounded. Her once-promising beauty was broken. The Princess looked like a dirty rat, for that is exactly what the woman thought of her.

The Princess spent her days responding to whatever task the woman gave her and collapsed into her straw-filled corner each evening.

The Princess's only pleasure was gathering berries in the woods. The best berries were near a clear pond, deep inside the forest. When her berry baskets were full, the Princess would wash and scrub her skin. It seemed an impossible task, for no matter how much dirt she removed, it seemed, there was always more, but the Princess worked at it with patience and precision. There was a particularly vexing patch of very brown skin just above her ankle, unusually shaped, and quite large, that the Princess rubbed until her skin stung. It was the only spot she could never remove.

When the water calmed from all her scrubbing, she would look at her reflection. She might look like a rat, but at least she wasn't as dirty.

For sixteen years, the Princess lived this life; the woman's hovel and opinion confined her as securely as a cage. Then, one day, the woman didn't wake up. The Princess wrapped the woman's body in the shabby blanket she always slept in and buried her under a tree.

A strange melancholy filled the Princess. The woman and her ways were all she knew. For days, she followed the routine, even without the woman's direction, until she ran out of supplies. There was no more grain to make mush, and no one else was there to replenish the supply.

The Princess had watched the woman take the long path into the village many times, but she was always forbidden to follow. She hesitated for some time at the edge of the path and finally determined to take it.

The village, in all its shades of grey and brown, was a mess of sound and smell. The Princess stood at the edge of the village. She watched as children ran with sticks, hooting while they weaved in and out of the busy buyers. Animals roamed, adding their noise to the streets. Hagglers raised their voices in increments, and the smell of fresh baked bread made the Princess's stomach ache.

"Who are you?" The young man's voice startled the Princess. She spun around to look at the voice, but she did not know what to say.

Another youth joined his companion. "Have you ever seen something so ugly in your life?"

"She looks like a rat." The other boy laughed.

"A dirty rat." They both laughed now, ribbing each other with elbows, as if priming themselves for further taunting.

The Princess turned from the boys. She wanted to run, but was soon surrounded by boys and girls alike.

"What is your name, rat girl?"

She still didn't know what to say. The woman had always called her "dirty rat." Was that her name? She said nothing.

"This girl is as stupid as a fish," a boy jeered.

As soon as the words left his mouth, the Princess's features reacted. Her cheeks puffed out and her eyes bulged, taking on the slow, stupid shine of a fish's eyes.

"Did you see that?!" a girl shrieked in wonder. "Her face changed."

"I think she's as stupid as a pig."

The Princess's rear end expanded so suddenly, she let out a squeal. The Princess grasped at her face and then her bottom.

What is happening to me? The thought raced through her mind, making her breath come in short, quick gasps. She ran back into the woods.

"Did you see that?" The youth all laughed loud and long over this surprise bit of entertainment.

The Princess ran straight to the pond. She stared at her refection in the water—her face and eyes looked swollen. She sat back, and her bottom felt big beneath her. Leaning forward, she splashed water on her face and scrubbed, hoping it would wash away, but it was as stubborn as the dark patch of skin above her ankle and would not be removed.

Her tears dropped down into the pond around her, and the water rippled outward with her sobs. "I am not a dirty rat. I am not a stupid fish. I am not a pig. Why is this happening to me?"

When night came, she collapsed on the straw in the corner of the hut, just as she had each night before. And just as it had each day before, the sun's morning light woke up the forest and dappled through the holes in the hovel's thatched roof. The Princess rubbed her eyes and stretched. Since she left the village without getting the grain she needed, picking berries was her first task. With no one to scold her for being slow, she walked leisurely to her favorite berry patch, listening to the birds in the trees. *If only human voices were as kind and beautiful*, she mused.

When her basket was finally full, the Princess looked around. She was alone, so she sat in the sun and tried to imitate the sounds the birds made. The sunlight fell in patches on the forest floor, mixing with the shade from thick, green leaves. The Princess popped a few berries in her mouth, closed her eyes, and smiled.

"Hello." The voice startled her. She jumped up, turning around and around to see where the voice had come from, but could see no one. A feeling of alarm jolted up her stomach and into her throat.

"Who's there?" she stammered.

"You have a beautiful singing voice," the voice replied instead of answering the question.

The Princess blushed and looked down. "You heard me?"

"Yes, I did. And it was lovely."

"Who are you?"

"A friend."

"What is a friend?" The word sounded awkward in the Princess's mouth.

"If you do not know, it's about time you had one. My name is George."

"I don't have a name," the Princess whispered.

"What? How can that be? You are almost grown and without a name?"

"The only thing I was ever called was 'dirty rat.'"

"What? That's awful and simply won't do. I will call you Robin because you can sing like a bird. That is, if it suits you?"

"Is a robin a bird?"

"Yes. There are robins and finches and starlings and jays, owls and crows; but I think Robin makes the best name for a girl. Do you like it?"

"I do. Robin is a good name. Thank you," said the Princess.

"You are most welcome," said George.

"Where are you? I can't see you." The Princess stood and walked toward the friendly voice.

"Don't bother trying to find me. I am an expert in hiding." George's voice came from the opposite side of the clearing now. The Princess jumped and whirled around.

"Why don't you want me to see you?" She approached the question with caution.

"I have my reasons." George's voice came from yet another location. The Princess spun around and squinted, scrutinizing the area the voice had come from.

"Come back tomorrow, and we can talk again," George paused, "friend."

"I will." The Princess's brows scrunched together. "Friend." She picked up the berry basket and walked home.

The Princess ate her berries in bed that night.

The next morning, she left so early the air still held a

chill. This time, she carried two baskets and picked berries for both she and George.

The Princess found the tree from the day before and waited. Morning passed, and it didn't look like George would come. She curled up in the afternoon sun and took a nap. When she awoke, she saw a plate with nuts and a little cake, and one of her berry baskets was gone. "George?"

"Right you are," said George.

"You came."

"Of course I came."

"Where are you, George? I want to see you."

"I know, but first, where did you find these berries? They are the best I've ever eaten."

"There is a place not far from here I like to go. I could show you where it is," said the Princess.

"I would love that."

The Princess jumped up and held out her hand.

George winced at the gesture. He sat in a thicket of brambles, his camouflage in place. The sticks and leaves he had woven together were strapped to his body. They concealed him, but poked and scratched his skin. He looked at his friend, then looked down. When he spoke, he made his voice sound as if he were on other side of the clearing. "Some other time."

"Why won't you let me see you? Are you a ghost or a toad or something?" The Princess grinned.

"No." It came out flat.

"Then let me see you. Come on. I'll take you to the best berry patch you have ever seen."

"No." It came out even flatter.

"Then I'd better go," said the Princess.

"No. Don't." It came out as a pleading blurt.

"Then let me see you. What harm can there be in that?"

"There can be a lot of harm," George said.

"Like what?"

"Robin, people can be very cruel if you don't look like them."

The Princess touched her swollen cheeks, "I know."

George was silent for some time, then whispered, "You probably do know, don't you?"

She heard a twig snap. She cautiously turned around. There was a young man about her age, stooping over a crutch with a bashful smile. His arms, back, and middle were covered with intertwined leaves and branches. On his head, he wore a hat that looked like the top of a bush.

"What is that?" The Princess pointed to George's unusual camouflage.

"See! I knew you wouldn't want to be my friend!"

"Of course I do!" she smiled. "Why wouldn't I? I've just never seen a shirt and hat made from forest branches, that's all."

George's eyes grew wide, then he laughed. "You mean this doesn't bother you?" He gestured down at his crippled body.

"No. Why would it?"

George unstrapped his stick shirt and hat and left them on the ground. His tunic was creased where the sticks had pushed in at his skin. He smiled a broad, genuine smile. "Now how about those berries. Please don't keep that place a secret from me any longer."

"Follow me," the Princess said.

They made their way slowly to the berry patch, laughing at George's attempted bird songs.

"Meet you tomorrow?" the Princess asked.

"Same tree?"

"Yes."

And so it was, every day until it rained.

The rain pelted the earth in angry bursts, and the air was gray and heavy. The Princess made her way to the tree, but George did not. She sat until she was soaked and shivering, then went out in search of her friend.

"George?" she called out again and again, but there was never any answer.

She continued well past dark. Lightning lit up the sky, followed by the deep rumble of thunder, which shook the mountain. She couldn't tell how far she had gone or where she was. She found shelter in a small crevice of the mountain and waited for the rain to stop.

"George!" she called out long and clear, but the rain and the thunder stopped the sound.

It was mid-afternoon of the next day before the rain stopped. The Princess was frantic. *Where is George? Perhaps he is hurt. I have to find him.* She ran through the trees looking for anything familiar, but there was nothing familiar to see.

"George!" It came out in an anxious burst.

The Princess was lost.

When she finally calmed her mind and controlled the movement of her breath, she realized her stomach was pitifully empty. She searched for something to eat while she continued to call out for George. It wasn't long before her apron pockets were filled with mushrooms, but George was still nowhere to be seen. She scanned the forest looking for a tree to sit under when she noticed a ragged, damp parchment hanging loosely from a nail on a tree.

She pulled it off the nail and stared at it. On the parchment was a drawing of a baby. And a very curious thing: on the baby's out-stretched leg, there was a brown mark above the ankle that looked just like the mark on her own leg. She stared at the parchment, wishing she could understand the other markings. Maybe George would know what they were. The Princess carefully placed the parchment in the pocket of her apron and continued looking for her friend.

It was almost dark when the Princess noticed smoke in the air. She followed it, careful to stay hidden in the shadows of the trees. She made her way around the perimeter of the fire until she could see the man sitting by it. He was old. His clothes matched the color of trees around him. He didn't have much to eat. She swallowed and said, "Hello."

"Who's there?"

"A friend."

"A friend. That would be a nice thing, indeed. Did you bring anything to eat?" He laughed. "We could have a dinner party."

"I have mushrooms," said the Princess.

"I have a fire. Come and join me, friend."

She did. She waited for him to call her a rat or fish or pig, but he did not. He called her Robin. She told him that was her name. They ate. She asked if he had seen a young man with a crutch, but he hadn't. Then he asked if she had any more food in her pockets.

"No, just this." She pulled out the parchment and opened it. "I found it on a tree. There is a picture of a baby on it." She showed the man.

"Oh ho! If you can find the girl in that picture, you would be rich."

"Rich? Why? Who is it?"

"The Princess, but she's not a baby anymore. King Seth has been posting these parchments throughout the kingdom every month for years."

"What happened to her?"

"A wicked fairy used her magic to steal the Princess, and no one has seen her since. That marking on the baby's leg is how they would recognize her. It's a birthmark, and a big one at that."

"A birthmark," the Princess said thoughtfully. Then looked up and said, "So the Princess was never found?"

"No. No, I don't believe she ever was. A mystery it is."

"Where does King Seth live?"

"You haven't seen the castle?" the man asked, astonished.

"No, it must be far from where I grew up."

"If you head east, at the edge of the forest, there is a road. That road winds up and around this mountain, and at the top, there is a castle like nothing you've ever seen."

When night descended, and she was sure the man was asleep, she pulled up her skirt to look at the mark she had tried to wash away so many times before. The firelight was low, but the large mark was unmistakable.

"I am a princess," she whispered in wonder. She stood up quietly and started through the woods. Using the light of the moon, she traveled in the direction the man had pointed.

"I am a princess." She said it again and again. "I have a father. I have a mother. My home is a castle. I am a princess. They will help me find George."

The Princess smiled at this new and startling thought; as she did, her chin softened and her teeth straightened. She could not see her body shift and change or feel her hair relax into chestnut curls. She did not notice her figure straighten. She thought only of finding the road to the castle and following it.

Most of the kingdom was still sleeping when she arrived at the castle gate. She showed the guard at the gate both the parchment and her leg. The guard sounded the trump and fell to the ground at her feet. "The lost Princess has returned!" He then stood, opened the gate, and escorted her in.

"You are not even going to check if my birthmark is real?"

"No, Your Highness."

"Why not?"

"I have no doubt," the guard said with confidence.

"No?" Just as she said it, she saw the King and Queen running out of the castle in their bed clothing. They looked at her with tears in their eyes and held her in their arms. The Queen whispered into her ear, "Ronwynn, I have missed you."

The King whispered into the other, "I hoped this day would come. You are home."

The Princess was so entirely dazed, she followed them into the castle. Ladies-in-waiting were leaping about, bringing in gowns, and two servants brought in a large mirror. The Princess gasped when she saw herself.

"What is wrong?" said the Queen.

"Don't you like it?" asked the King.

"I don't usually look like that," the Princess said as she pointed to herself in the mirror. "I look like you, Mother. I . . . I don't understand. My reflection in the pond didn't look anything like this." She gestured at her tall and elegant frame.

It came out simply and with stark realization from both parents: "The curse."

The King and Queen told her the story. The curse. The search. The heartache.

The Princess told them her story, but stopped at the part about George. "We have to find him!" she said with urgency. "He may be hurt."

How could the King and Queen deny their sweet daughter anything when she had suffered so much? A carriage and food were prepared, and they headed to the woods in search of George.

It took time, but the Princess found George.

"Robin, I've been searching the forest for you."

"And I you."

"You look different."

"Better?" the Princess asked.

"You look like I imagined you the first time I heard your voice," he said with a smile. The Princess smiled, too.

"Who are all these people?" said George.

"This is the King and Queen," said the Princess, pointing at her parents.

"What?"

"They are my parents. It's a long story. Would you like to hear it? You can join me at the castle."

"The castle? Really?"

"Yes. It is magnificent."

And so it was that the two friends found themselves living in the castle.

The King and Queen doted on their daughter, day and night, in an effort to make up for the many years they had missed her. In spite of all they could offer their princess, the King was not satisfied. Her story stirred up an anger inside him that could not be extinguished. The thought of her spending her youth looking like a dirty rat—being used, teased, and taunted—made him toss and turn at night.

The King called for the royal carriage and said to his daughter, "I would like you to take us to the village you grew up in."

"I don't know if I can find my way," said the Princess.

"I would like you to try, my dear."

They spent some time on bumpy trails, but the royal family, accompanied by George and all their escorts, finally found the village. When the King and Queen saw the hovel their daughter grew up in, the Queen cried. The King's fists clenched. They sent the trumpeters to gather the villagers. It was an unnecessary action, as the villagers were already gathered, staring at the carriage and royal family in wonder.

"This is the Princess Ronwynn," the King announced to the people. "She spent her youth in this village and was treated poorly. We are angry at the way you treated her, and you will be punished. As her first royal decree, we will let the Princess Ronwynn decide your punishment."

The Princess looked at her father in surprise.

"Whatever punishment you feel is just will stand, darling." The King smiled at his daughter.

The people of the village looked at her with fear in their

eyes. They did not recognize her and could not remember how they treated her. The Princess looked at her mother. The Queen looked just as surprised as the Princess felt. She looked at her father; he stood staring at the people who had done her harm, jaw tight, fists clenched. The Princess loved him for it, but she knew what she must do.

"Whatever I feel is just would be fine with you, Father?"

"Yes. You name the punishment, and I swear it shall be done," said the King.

All eyes were upon the Princess as she began. "My father is angry with the way I was treated here, but I am not. It was not an easy life growing up here, but I would not trade what I have learned from my experience. I was left here as a small baby, and a woman took me in. I did not know who I was, and neither did you, but inside each of us is greatness. I hope we can treat those around us as if they are much more than what they appear. Let us all treat each other with kindness and respect."

"Well said, darling," the Queen smiled.

Now it was the King's turn to look surprised. His fists unclenched, and his jaw relaxed. He reached out and held his daughter's hand. "It seems the castle is not the only place to learn to be a wise ruler," he whispered.

George started clapping. The people of the village joined him.

The Princess smiled at George, the people, and then her parents. "My story started with a celebration; let us end it with one, too."

"Agreed. The lost Princess has returned! There is no better reason to celebrate than that," exclaimed the King.

"You are all invited to the castle in one week's time for a fine feast and dancing," the Princess announced to the people of the village.

The people of the village cheered.

In the castle's great room, music and the sweet smell of rich food filled the air. The Princess stood with George by her side, welcoming each person into the castle ballroom. Some were clad in worn, brown tones, others in fine gowns and suits, but all were warmly welcomed into the castle.

When the people tired of dancing and eating, the Princess told them her story. It was quite a spectacle. Shadow puppets and colored lights, music and voice, all combined in great artistry to show the Princess's transformation from dirty rat to royalty.

And it all ended well, for from that time forth, the curse was celebrated as a gift.

A REAL PRINCESS

There once was a royal family who lived in a time of fairy-tale beginnings and happily-ever-afters, who happened to find themselves in a very messy middle.

After entertaining fourteen suitors in eighteen days, the Princess exclaimed, "How can I possibly know which prince will love me all the way through Ever After, happily?"

The Princess's only escape was reading a good book. One day, she was on the balcony reading when the kingdom's resident dragon swooped overhead. *Resident Dragon* makes him sound quaint and likable, but in reality, he wasn't a pleasant resident at all. The dragon was green and graceful, with purple spikes, long claws, and even bigger jaws. He had very sensitive nostrils and an appetite for princesses.

Before she even knew he was there, the dragon snatched her up. The Princess screamed, though it was only partly out of fear and mostly out of wonder. Viewing the kingdom from this aerial perspective was fascinating. Flying was a real adventure—until the dragon plunged into the dark and tangled undergrowth of the wild woods.

These were the kind of woods that inspired knights to practice their defensive maneuvers daily. The kind of woods that made fair maidens faint and gave children endless fodder for nightmares.

The dragon deposited the Princess in his stony cave, next to what looked suspiciously like a cooking fire.

The Princess tried to remember what princesses were apt to do in books when faced with a horrid dragon. *Isn't a knight in shining armor supposed to come to my rescue?* She looked out the cave's entrance, but there was not a knight to be found. *I guess not.*

The Princess did the only thing she could think of—she swooned, "Please, don't eat me."

The dragon smiled, showing every one of his sharp, white teeth.

Now the Princess was genuinely concerned.

"What do you plan to do with me?" she asked, trembling.

The dragon's black, forked tongue flicked out and around his lips.

"I was afraid of that," the Princess groaned.

The dragon nudged her closer to the fire with the back of his fingers, his long claws scraping the ground.

The Princess quickly side-stepped his fingers and

backed up against the cave wall. She slumped to the ground, watching the dragon. Then, she did something she never thought she would do. Something she never thought she *could* do. Something she *had* to do. It was her only option.

She took off her shoes.

There in the cave, she revealed something she had been trying to keep a secret her whole life: her very large, very smelly feet.

The dragon's sensitive nostrils flared. He coughed, sputtered, and with a thud, dropped to the ground. The Princess, seeing her small window for escape, slipped out of the cave and ran barefoot into the woods.

Meanwhile, a knight all shining in armor, was on his way to save the Princess. As he rode toward the dragon's cave, he practiced possible opening lines. "Fear not, fair maiden! I have come to save thee." "Dastardly dragon, unhand that princess!" "Don't worry. I'm handsome, I'm strong, and I know how to deal with dragons."

The Knight and the Princess, preoccupied with their own thoughts, nearly collided on the trail. The Knight looked at the Princess; she was stunning, but dragon-less. Slightly puzzled, he said, "Fear not, Fair Princess, I have come to rescue you."

The Princess smiled at the Knight. "I don't really need to be rescued, but I could use a ride home."

The Knight took off his helmet, and his dark hair swooped to the side. He was magnificent. "Why yes, of course," he said in a chivalrous tone. He held out his hand to hoist the Princess onto his horse. Her foot swung up and over the horse's back.

The smell was powerful.

The Knight's eyes began to water. His trusty white steed whinnied and shuffled uncomfortably. The Knight hadn't practiced any lines for this. He was brave enough to combat a dragon, but not kind enough to overlook smelly feet.

"Did the dragon curse you with those horrible feet instead of eating you?" said the Knight, coughing.

"No."

"You *are* a princess, right?"

"Yes," the Princess said, folding her arms defensively.

"I didn't know Princesses were capable of such . . . stinkiness."

"You don't *have* to give me a ride home," said the Princess.

"Really?" the Knight said, relieved.

"Oooh." The Princess hopped off his horse in disgust. She stomped through the tangled wood toward the castle gates.

When the King and Queen saw the Princess, they cried out, "Oh darling, we're so glad you're safe. We saw the dragon take you. We were just coming to find you."

"That dragon must have been awful," said the Queen.

"Where is the Knight? Did he . . . uh . . . get eaten?" asked the King.

"Oooh, I wish," said the Princess.

"What?"

"The dragon was fine. It was the Knight who was horrid," the Princess cried.

Her parents hurried her into the castle, where they all sat together. "What happened, darling?" her parents coaxed.

"I had to think of a way to stop the dragon from eating me, so I took off my shoes. It was awful, but it worked. I escaped and started running toward the castle. That's when I bumped into the Knight. He was handsome and chivalrous and hoisted me up on his horse, then he turned green—literally, green. He didn't want to give me a ride home because . . . of my feet. He didn't even think I was a real princess!" She sobbed a long deep sob. "No one is ever going to want to marry a princess with stinky feet."

"There will be a wonderful man, willing and wanting to marry you, with your feet exactly the way they are," said the King.

"No, there won't!"

The King smiled at the Queen. The Queen smiled back at him, and then at their daughter.

"Oh, I wouldn't be so sure about that," said the Queen, as she unlaced her shoes to reveal even larger, even smellier feet.

The Princess gasped and plugged her nose, "Mom!?"

Then her eyes opened wide, and she hugged her father. "Dad!" He was much more than a King now . . . he was a hero.

The King looked at his precious daughter and said, "You are charming, smart, and beautiful, and the only man who deserves to marry you is one who can look . . . and smell . . . past your feet."

THE PRINCESS
WHO COULD FLY

There once was a princess who could fly.

She grew up like every other princess, with her feet on the cold, stone floor of a castle. But when she was eleven years old, two things happened: her parents died, and she opened a box.

The first was a sad affair. The King and Queen took ill and never recovered. They left the Princess too early, and the whole kingdom mourned their loss.

The second: the box. Without the box, we wouldn't have this story.

The wooden box was ornate with beautifully carved birds in flight and inlaid with gold. It was presented to the Princess as a parting gift from her mother and father.

The last words her father said were, "Trust this gift."

Her mother added, "And know that we love you."

For many days, the Princess couldn't see through her tears long enough to open the box; she could only hold it tight to her chest. But the inevitable day came when the sobs subsided, and she opened the box.

The lid was a tight fit. She pried hard with her fingers, and finally, the top popped open, still attached by two hinges in the back. Music began to play from within the box. The Princess smiled in recognition; it was the song her mother always sang to her.

> *Some have the gift of laughter that brightens*
>   *up a space.*
> *Some have the gift of light that chases dark*
>   *away.*
> *Oh my child, my lovely child,*
> *If you seek your gift you'll find it.*
> *Then a joy will fill your precious heart,*
> *And cause your soul to fly.*
> *It will cause your soul to fly.*
> *Fly, fly, my princess, fly,*
> *Fly, fly, my princess, fly.*

The Princess cradled the box and danced to the music the same way her mother did when she sang to her. When the music stopped, she looked inside the box. There, nestled in black velvet, was a small piece of parchment with a question scrawled across it. *Can you fly?*

This question filled her mind with memories of her father.

She was on top of the bed. Many multicolored pillows were stacked in a wobbly pile, and she stood at the top. Her parents walked in. Her mother rushed to the bed and exclaimed, "What are you doing?"

But her father just smiled and asked, "Can you fly?"

"I want to fly!" she said, then jumped. She fell, a cascade of fine silk and stiff petticoats, then hit the bed. The tower of pillows tumbled and buried her first attempt at flight.

"Oh darling, are you all right?" her mother said, throwing pillows from the bed. Her mother's tone suggested a scolding was coming, but it never came, because when her mother found her, she was giggling.

"That wasn't flying, but it sure was fun!" she exclaimed.

"Whatever gave you the idea to fly?" her mother asked.

"I was hoping that was my special gift, like in the song."

"Oh?"

"And Father told me I have to look for my gift, and only I can find it, but when I do, it will make me feel like I can fly. So I thought maybe my special gift was to fly."

"I see," her mother said and smiled. "I see."

"I guess I'll have to try some other things out, though. I'm not sure I can fly."

"You can do anything you believe you can do," said her father, twirling her in the air.

"I think I'll try embroidery next."

The Princess remembered trying embroidery and how it frustrated her fingers. Then she tried singing, but the song felt like a rock in her throat. Musical instruments did not sound musical in her hands. Painting made her feel panicky. Cooking ended in catastrophe. After all these failures, her parents continued to urge her to keep trying. "You'll find your gift." They said it with such confidence she believed them, but now they were gone.

The Princess slumped into a high-backed chair, facing the portrait of her parents. "How can I ever rule the kingdom? I am just a little girl. I'm not extraordinary in any way. How could you leave me?"

The Princess woke the next morning with a stiff neck and puffy eyes. She had slept the night in the chair. She picked up the box laying at her feet and placed it on her lap. She opened it and let the music lift her heavy heart, then she read the parchment once again. *Can you fly?*

"I want to," she said aloud to the portrait in front of her. "I want to."

Can you fly? The question was perplexing. She had never heard of anyone flying before. Why would her father ask such a silly question? Did he know something she did not?

What would he want the answer to be? She whispered, "Yes, I can fly."

I can fly. The words wriggled in her mind like a little caterpillar tickling her thoughts.

Many months passed as the Princess opened the box and repeated the words. "I can fly." This statement, now like a butterfly, flitted about in the Princess's mind.

I can fly.

One bright, blue-sky afternoon, the Princess opened her box in the garden. She closed her eyes and listened to the music. When she opened her eyes again, she discovered she was no longer on the ground, but floating in the air. The Princess hung in the air, suspended and surprised. After taking a long deep breath, she moved slowly, tentatively, through the air. With a slight movement to the left or right, she could propel herself in any direction.

The Princess soon found flying was like swimming, but it took less effort. She smiled, and up she flew. She touched the tops of the trees and continued upward until she felt the moisture of clouds on her face. She swooped down, breathing in the wonderful, sharp scent of pine as she skimmed the tops of the trees.

"I can fly!" She spun in the air laughing.

She flew up and over the castle to see her kingdom from the air. She flew so high her kingdom looked like a patchwork quilt, with dark green forests stitched side-by-side with light green valleys. She flew low, so she could hover and rest in the thick trees surrounding her kingdom. While hidden from view, she could observe the individual subjects of her kingdom as they went about their daily routines. She flew home, and as she descended, stepping down to the ground, she said, "So this is what it feels like to find your gift."

Every day, just before lunch, the Princess flew for the pure pleasure of it.

After lunch, she planned to hear her people's petitions and grievances, just as her parents had. But the head advisor sniffed, "You are just a pretty little princess. Let the problems of the kingdom be solved by someone with more experience and wisdom."

These words stung like an annoying insect. The Princess straightened. "I am the ruler of this kingdom, no matter how young or pretty I am, and I will rule it as my father and mother did before me. Send the people in."

It was a powerful statement—more powerful, perhaps, than she actually felt—but it would do. She sat on the throne and summoned the first petitioner.

An old woman approached, wearing layers of brown and smelling of earth. She was holding a fat hen. The woman's sunken eyes widened to see the young Princess sitting on the throne.

The Princess cleared her throat and said, "I invite you to tell me your name and your grievances." It was what her father and mother used to say.

"My name is Hilda," the woman said. "I once had ten beautiful hens, and now I have only one because of my rotten son. I offered him a choice: he could take the chickens to market to sell, or the eggs. The senseless boy thought the chickens would fetch a better price and took all but one to market. He did bring home a fair amount of money, but now we only have one chicken."

"You are holding the chicken now," the Princess observed.

"Yes. Now the boy wants to sell the eggs from this chicken. And do I see any of the money? No. Unfair, don't you think?" She looked at the Princess.

The Princess didn't know what to say, so she didn't say anything; she just waited for the woman to continue. It didn't take long.

"He has taken everything from me and gives nothing back. He continues to take, take, take. I only have one hen. I don't even have enough for me, but he wants all the money he can get so he can set up house for his little wife. It won't be long before I have nothing and she has everything. I want justice!"

This final demand startled the Princess. She was so absorbed in the story she wasn't prepared for it. "What would you have me to do?" she asked.

"Punish him."

The Princess sat on the throne, wordless, for an uncomfortably long time. Finally, she looked up, but instead of pronouncing a judgment, she asked a question. "May I show you something, Hilda?"

"What is it?"

"Let go of your chicken, and come with me." The Princess got down off her throne and began to walk outside.

Hilda held tight to her chicken. "Where are you going?" She followed the Princess outside.

"You'll have to let go of your chicken," the Princess reminded.

Hilda tensed. "Where are you taking me?"

"Let go of the chicken, take my hand, and I'll show you."

The Princess knew she could fly, but was unsure if what she was about to try would even work. She took Hilda's hand (and a deep breath) and ascended into the sky. Hilda's mouth hung open and speechless. She gripped the Princess's arm until the two came to rest in the branches of a tree, and the Princess said simply, "Watch the cottage."

It wasn't long before they heard the squalling of a baby. Then, other youthful, demanding voices added their complaints to the baby's loud cries. Suddenly, the door opened, and there was a mother, with a babe in arms and four boys of varying heights pulling at her skirts.

Hilda scoffed, "That's a miserable existence."

The mother below them sat down on the grass outside her cottage, soothing the baby with milk and the boys with a song.

Hilda looked at all the boys surrounding their mother and sighed. "That is what I always wanted. Look at all those strong boys who love their mother. I only got one who doesn't love me a bit."

They watched as the mother taught her young sons to care for the garden and the animals. They also watched as the mother scolded, redirected, and became exasperated with her boys when they did not complete the tasks she had given them.

All the while, Hilda vacillated between wanting and

not wanting that which was not hers to have, but hers to observe.

When they returned to the castle, the hen's fearful clucking welcomed them. Hilda picked up the frightened bird and soothed it. She smiled at the Princess. "I see what must be done."

"You do?" The Princess couldn't hide her surprise.

"Yes." Hilda laughed, then said, "You are a rather extraordinary princess." And with that, Hilda left. The Princess was unsure what conclusion Hilda had come to, but she was happy Hilda left knowing what to do—and even happier knowing she would not have to punish Hilda's son for taking what his mother offered him.

The next time the Princess shared her gift of flight, it was with two young shepherds who came to share their complaints. They could barely stifle their argument long enough to greet the Princess.

The Princess looked at the young men, not much older than herself, and said, "I invite you to tell me your names and your grievances."

"I am Hans." Hans hardly got the second word out before the other shepherd interjected, "I am Dieter. He wants to bring *his* sheep to pasture on *my* hillside."

"It isn't your hillside," Hans interrupted. "You cannot own a hillside."

"If he takes *his* sheep on *my* hillside, there won't be enough food for my sheep."

"There is plenty of food for both our flocks, and it is

NOT your hillside!"

"I was there first!"

Sounding much like bleating sheep, they continued talking over each other about the particular conveniences of the disputed hillside.

After some time, the Princess interrupted. "What would you have me do to assist you?"

"Tell him to leave *my* hillside alone!"

"Tell him it is not *his* hillside, and *my* sheep can graze there, too!"

The Princess stifled a smile, for she knew just what they needed to see. "Come with me." She walked to the courtyard without a word. The shepherds were so stunned with her action, they followed her. "Take hold of my hands." They each grabbed for the same hand, and a battle of expressions ensued until Hans backed down and took the other hand. When the Princess started to rise, both boys let out a yelp.

"Just hold on, and you will be fine. I do this every day."

The shepherds were too astonished to say anything else, and the Princess was glad for the quiet. She flew them to a hillside and asked, "Is this the hillside in question?"

Hans said, "The very one."

Dieter whispered, "It looks so large when you can see it all at once."

The Princess turned and flew in the opposite direction.

"Where are you taking us?" they both asked, with obvious concern in their voices.

"You must see something." She flew toward a neighboring kingdom. The three of them sat on the branch of a tree overlooking a grassy hillside below.

This hillside was much smaller and held no less than seven shepherds and all their sheep. The sheep were grazing, and the shepherds were singing, laughing, and telling stories. The shepherds looked like they actually enjoyed tending sheep. When it came time to gather and count the sheep, they worked together.

"I've never seen sheep gathered so quickly," Dieter muttered.

"Would you like to see more?" asked the Princess.

"No," they both said in soft tones.

Before they crossed the border into their own kingdom, Dieter looked at Hans and said, "Do you know any songs?"

"Sure. My father taught me all the songs he knew."

"Why don't you join me on the hillside tonight, and you can teach them to me."

"All right."

The shepherd boys were quiet when they left the castle. Their sheep, on the other hand, were loud and demanded their immediate attention.

It wasn't long afterward that stories began to spread over the kingdom like a soft blanket. Stories of a young princess who could fly, and who ruled the kingdom with such wisdom and compassion that all would prosper during her reign.

THE STORY TREE

In an old mountain village, deep in the center of the woods, there was a tree as wide as a house and so tall— so tall the children could only guess where it touched the sky.

Every day, the children of the village would gather around the tree and sing:

Story tree, oh, story tree, tell a story to me.
Story tree, oh, story tree, tell a story to me.

And the tree would begin, "Once upon a time . . . " and spin stories for the children like gossamer cloth.

One day, a little girl came to the tree alone. She looked at the tree through her tears and sang:

Story tree, oh, story tree, tell a story to me.
Story tree, oh, story tree, I need a story to hold me.

But this time, the tree did not tell a story. Instead it asked a question, "Why do you need a story to hold you?"

"My grandmother died," the girl answered.

"Tell me about your grandmother, child."

"I could talk to my grandmother about anything. I could tell her about my dreams, even if they were scary. I could tell her about how I hate my new shoes because they don't fit right. I miss her saggy cheeks and her soft lap."

"I can see that you loved her."

"Yes." The child paused. "Will you tell me a story?"

The tree waited a long time before responding. "I will tell you a story, child, but this time, you must close your eyes and keep them closed."

The little girl wiped her eyes then closed them tight. When she did, a woman as old as earth emerged from deep in the hollow of the tree. The woman's body was twisted and gnarled, her skin rough and brown, like the bark of a tree. The silver wisps of her hair hung like spider's webs around her shoulders. She smelled of wild herbs and rotting wood.

The woman wanted to wipe the tears from the girl's face, but as she approached the girl, an ugly voice in her mind said, *You will scare her.*

The woman shrunk back. *But the child's eyes are closed. She won't see me; she will only see the marvelous pictures in her mind, created by the story.* The old woman spoke, and it wasn't long before they were both lost in the cadence of "Once upon a time."

As the words fell from her mouth, the woman gently wrapped her arms around the girl. When at last the story rounded the corner into "happily ever after," the child said, "I told you."

"What did you tell me?"

"A story *can* hold you." The girl smiled, comforted.

"Yes, I think you were right about that, child."

"May I open my eyes now?"

"No, you mustn't," said the old woman. She was sure she would scare the child.

"Please? You feel so real to me. I want to see." The girl's face was so earnest the old woman forgot to listen to the fear inside her.

"All right." The words fluttered out like bird's wings.

The little girl opened her eyes and stared. "You're not a tree." Her face brightened into a smile. "You're a grandmother!"

The old woman stopped and wondered how words so unfamiliar could sound so right.

"Come with me. Come to the village with me. You can be a grandmother at my house."

"No. No, I cannot do that child. They won't see me as you see me." The old woman left the child standing alone as she backed into her tree.

"Please?"

But the woman was hidden in the tree as she always had been before.

The girl went back to the village and gathered the children to tell them the story tree's secret. The children came again, gathered around the tree, and sang:

Story tree, oh, story tree, tell a story to me.
Story tree, oh, story tree, tell a story to me.

The tree began, "Once upon a time . . ."
But the children were not done singing.

Story tree, oh, story tree, tell a story to me.
Story tree, oh, story tree—our grandmother we
would like you to be.

The old woman said, "This is something that cannot be."

"Why not?"

"It just can't be. But I'll tell you a story." The children all settled under the tree and listened.

The old woman wove a beautiful story around them. At the end of the story, the children's voices were soft. "Grandmother, please come to the village with us, please."

"No," she sighed.

But . . . day after day the children came and sang, and hoped, and listened. And whether it took a week, a month, or a year, no one is quite sure—but this much I can tell you . . .

Stories are no longer found deep in the center of the woods, but in the heart of the village, where they belong.

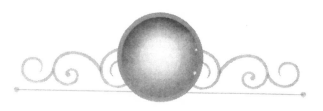

MOONSTONES
AND MAGIC

Sun splashed through the stained-glass window. Each and every color glowed both bright and beautiful. Catherine traced the metal outline of the glass with her finger.

She let her eyes wander across the room, relishing the colored light and patterns the stained glass made as the sun's rays shone through it. The stained-glass window was her favorite of all the gifts her father had brought home. He had commissioned it in memory of her mother. Its beauty eased the grief they both felt in her absence.

Bong! Bong! Bong!

The bell. Catherine ran out the door—her father was home.

She met him on the shore; that was her way. She knew he had a present for her hidden under his hat; that was his way. They embraced, and he kissed her on the top of the head and said, "Hold out your hands and close your eyes." She smiled and did as he asked. He removed his hat and placed a moonstone necklace in her hands. "You can open your eyes now."

Catherine opened her eyes and stared at the necklace in her hands. "It's beautiful!"

"Yes, just like you."

The stone, a soft white color, was a rounded circle mounted on a silver chain. "It reminds me of the moon."

"Clever girl, it is called a moonstone." Catherine put it around her neck.

"Thank you, father. I love it!"

"You'll love it even more when I tell you the story behind it."

"There is a story, too?"

"Oh, yes. I'll tell it to you after supper tonight."

Later that evening, Catherine listened, captivated by her father's tales of adventure. He touched the moonstone hanging from her neck. "I was in a land far, far away in a market place. There were people packed into the streets so tightly you could barely move from one place to the other. I was looking for a treasure for you when I spotted a man selling jewelry. I thought to myself, *Catherine is old enough now to appreciate jewelry, I will look and see if there is something she would like.*" Catherine blushed. She had turned twelve years old while he was away. "I looked at all kinds of gems and beads, but stopped when I saw this.

It reminded me of the moon—just like it did you—and so I inquired about it. The old merchant told me it was a moonstone and had magical powers."

"Magical powers, really?"

"Yes. It is said that during a full moon, you can place the stone under your tongue and see the future."

"Do you really think the story is true?"

"We'll have to wait and see. The next full moon is just a few days away."

"Will you be here to see it with me?"

"No, my darling. I am off tomorrow once again."

Catherine looked down to hide her disappointment.

"But, I will be back in one week with enough money to stay for several months, maybe even a year."

"Really?" Her face brightened.

"Really." He smiled. "One more story, then off to bed."

After a long goodnight from her father, Catherine held the moonstone in her hand, letting the images of her father's stories play in her mind as she fell asleep.

The next morning, she sent her father off with kisses, a book she loved, and no tears; it was her way. He left her with a seashell for each day he would be gone and an extra-long embrace; it was his way.

As his ship set sail from the docks, he called out, "Don't forget, the full moon is in three days. When I come home, I want to hear all about the future."

She smiled and called back, "I won't forget." Catherine placed the shells in a velvet bag and held the moonstone hanging from her neck. She wanted to cry but held the tears in with the thought, *Next time he comes home, he will stay for a year.*

Three days passed, and Catherine sat at her bedroom window, waiting for the moon. She was wrapped in a blanket and holding the moonstone, gazing at the stars. When the full moon was perfectly framed in her window, she placed the moonstone under her tongue and closed her eyes, waiting to see visions of the future. All she saw was blackness. She smiled and went to bed thinking up grand ideas to weave into stories of the future that she would tell her father when he got back home.

That night, Catherine had a dream. A woman walked into her room wearing a gown bearing the soft, silver glow of the moon. She was elegant and looked powerful. Catherine whispered, "Who are you?"

"Catherine, I am your destiny."

'You know my name?"

"Oh, yes, child. I know your name and everything that has happened to you in your twelve short years. I also know everything that will happen to you." The woman smiled at Catherine's surprise.

"You can see my future? Will you tell me about it?"

"That I cannot do, but I can give you a choice."

"What is it?"

"Would you rather have joy and contentment in your youth and misery in your old age, or misery in your youth and joy and contentment in your old age?"

Catherine thought for a moment. "I choose joy and contentment in old age, as I will have many more years of that than I will of youth."

"And so it shall be." The woman smiled—a kind, gentle smile—and was gone.

Catherine awoke and looked around the room. *What a strange dream.*

Over the next week, Catherine put a shell on the sill of the stained glass window daily. When she placed the last shell, Catherine smiled; her father should be home soon. A full day passed, and her father did not come home. Catherine sighed, removed her shoes and stockings, and walked toward the sea. She loved the feel of soft sand beneath her feet and the smell of salt in the air. She picked up a shell, cleaned the grit off in the sea, and stood for some time letting the waves wash over her feet and ankles.

Day after day, she scanned the sea for her father's ship, and night after night, she added a shell to her collection. When the shells filled the window sill, she placed them on the floor below.

Bong! Bong! Bong!

Catherine ran for the door; her father was home. But when she got to the door, there was a large man with dark, cold eyes standing in the doorway. He was shouting instructions to the servants to gather up the household.

When the entire household was gathered, the man stood in front of the stained glass, making him appear as a dark silhouette. His voice was loud and harsh, "The master of this house has perished at sea along with his great wealth. You are all dismissed. This estate will be under new ownership in the morning."

No one moved.

"Perhaps you did not understand me. You have no more employment here. Go away," he boomed. The servants all hurried away, leaving Catherine alone in the room crying.

"What are you still doing here?" his voice barked.

"The master of this house was my father. What do I do?"

"That is not my concern."

The servants were gone before Catherine could see clearly enough through her tears to gather a few things. The words *What do I do?* pounded in her mind like a rhythm. Catherine found herself wandering through the village, not sure what she would eat or where she would live. She observed the people of the village carefully. The sights, sounds, and smells of the village were unfamiliar to Catherine. The servants had always carried out the household business in the village.

Perhaps there is someone in need of my service, who would offer me a place to stay and food to eat, she thought as she scanned the crowd. A mother carrying a squalling baby, hefting two baskets of food, and followed by three children caught Catherine's eye. She approached the woman and asked, "May I be of assistance?"

The woman looked at Catherine with surprise in her eyes, then handed Catherine the baby and said, "Follow me."

Catherine followed her to a simple home just outside the village. The woman opened the door and shooed her children inside. She took the now quiet baby from Catherine's arms and said, "Thank you. I'm sure you need to be getting home now."

Catherine looked down; her mother was gone, her father was gone, and now her home was gone. The woman was about to close the door when Catherine said, "I could stay with you and help you with your children if you can give me food and shelter."

"We barely have enough food and shelter for ourselves." The baby erupted again in loud, unhappy screams. The woman sighed, "You may sleep on the floor and eat whatever is left when my children have had their fill."

For many years, Catherine cared for the children of this household. The floor never felt as soft as her bed at home, and she rarely had enough food to feel full, but she had the love of the children she cared for, her moonstone, and a hope the dream she dreamt was real. Her youth would be filled with pain and sorrow, but, in the end, she would have joy and contentment.

The children of the household grew, but even as they did, they never stopped clambering for Catherine's stories. And so it was they cried and pleaded with their parents to let her stay, when their father came home one day with empty hands and announced there was not enough to feed an extra mouth any longer.

"There is a rich merchant in town who has been

inquiring about a tutor for his children. I have made arrangements for you to work for him. He can give you a bed, more food, and clothing. You will be better off in his care."

"Thank you." Catherine held back the sob in her throat. *A bed cannot replace the love I have for these children.* She kept her thought concealed and showed her gratitude with a stoic smile.

And so it was, Catherine found herself in a house not much different than the one she used to live in, with a boy and a girl to care for and teach. She even had a bed to sleep in.

The girl folded her arms at the sight of Catherine. "I do not need to learn anything. Especially from someone like you."

The boy ran around and around the room, never stopping long enough to say anything.

"Do you like stories?" Catherine smiled.

"Probably not."

"Well, I will tell you one anyway." And Catherine began to tell a story of a young girl who had everything, but one day it was all taken away when her father died and their fortune was gone. She filled the story with such wonderful characters and details the girl listened. The boy continued to run around and around, but when the story came to an end he asked, "What did the father do to make money?"

The girl asked, "What was the book the girl missed the most?"

74

Catherine smiled. *Questions are the beginning to an education* was what her tutor had always taught her. She felt content with her small success.

Over the next several years, Catherine continued to work with the boy and girl. They did not like her. They did not like to learn. Catherine enjoyed the comforts of a fine feather bed, but she didn't sleep well. The worries she had for the children kept her awake like a story without an ending. She comforted herself with the knowledge that she had food to eat, her moonstone, and a hope that as she got older, things would get better.

Catherine was surprised when the master of the house told her she was no longer needed. He was not pleased with his children's progress in their education.

Catherine was once again forced to look for a way to care for herself. She was plenty old enough now to work for money. She soon found, however, there were not many jobs women could do. She took the one job she could: washing clothing for the King and his court.

She spent every day scrubbing next to three other women. Her hands were soon rough and cracked, and her back ached, but she had enough money to buy food for herself and was allowed to sleep in the small building provided for the servants.

One day, Catherine told a story to combat the tedium of the task before her. The other women she worked with smiled. They continued to scrub as she spun tales, and they listened. For some time, she was quite content.

Unfortunately, the mistress of the laundry put an end to her storytelling one afternoon with a single, but final pronouncement. "There is to be no more talking in here; just scrubbing."

The silence intensified the strong smell of soap and the complete monotony of the task, but in time, Catherine grew to love the rhythm of washing. She chose to feel satisfaction knowing she did not do the job alone, and in the end, the clothes were clean. Catherine held fast to the thought that it was only in her youth she would suffer so. In her old age, she would have joy and contentment. Occasionally, in the dark of night when sleep would just not come, Catherine wondered how long youth lasted. It had been twenty-three years since her father died and she felt her youth had already slipped away in the daily work of earning enough to eat.

One evening, she made her way to the marketplace with her meager earnings to purchase food. The bit of bread she could buy was a welcome relief from the constant tang of soap. The marketplace was more crowded than usual, and there were many unfamiliar faces. She enjoyed the variety this new scene provided. Out of the corner of her eye, she saw a horse rear up and throw its rider. The horse stomped the ground, then ran, filling the air with the sound of hoof beats. Men dressed in fine clothes jumped up to chase it. Catherine did not see the rider, but the horse was now heading straight for her. She held out her hands in a gesture to both calm the animal and protect herself, but the horse knocked her down, reared up, and landed on her arm. She felt the bone break and cried out in pain.

The men continued after the horse, and Catherine was left in the street. She made her way back to the castle to seek attention for her arm. A doctor wrapped it tight and told her she would be fine, but it would take a few months to heal. She thanked him, but indicated she didn't have money to pay for his services. He smiled and said, "I'll just take that unusual necklace from you, and that will be payment enough."

Catherine was so stunned she couldn't say anything.

The doctor looked at her with annoyance. "Are you going to pay me, or shall I call the guards?"

Catherine struggled with her one good arm to remove the moonstone necklace. The doctor helped it off and was on his way. When Catherine arrived at the washing station, she found the head mistress had already replaced her. "We'll need your bed tonight," was all she said.

Catherine left the castle in search of shelter and food in the woods. It was a difficult task to gather berries from thorny, wild bushes with just one good arm. For weeks, she could never quite manage to find enough to eat, and soon, hunger clouded her mind. Catherine tried to hold on to any comforting thoughts, but she was just too tired and hungry.

While gathering berries one day, Catherine found a ball of warp yarn laying on the ground. It was damp from the forest floor, but it was a beautiful and unusual color; the same bluish-purple of the sky at dusk. Certainly, someone in the town would trade this for some food.

She approached the market stalls. The smells made her stomach yearn for food. The people in the market place stared at her and pointed to the yarn she was carrying. She could hear the whispers circulating, but was too tired to listen. She lifted the ball of warp yarn, offering it to the man selling bread, his eyes widened when he saw it. He smiled broadly and said, "For that ball of yarn, you can have the pick of my wares." Before she could make her choice, the voices of other sellers distracted her. "I will give you twice what he offers, come to my stall!"

"Don't be a fool. I'll give you all the food you can eat in exchange for your treasure." She looked at the ball of warp yarn, confused at the commotion it was causing.

A young boy with dirty hands and a round face tugged at her skirt. "Mother, Mother," he said with urgency. "Come with me."

Catherine was truly perplexed. It felt as though she were in a dream. "You must be mistaken, I am not your mother."

"Come with me!" He yanked so hard on her dress it nearly ripped.

Seeing his great anxiety, she left the stall and followed the child. She knelt beside him. "What is it, little one?"

"That ball of yarn. The King wants it. The King will give you enough gold to make you rich. Take it to the castle."

"What? Why would the King want a ball of warp yarn?"

"I don't know," the boy said.

"Seems a silly thing. Is this just a story?"

"No." The boy smiled and ran away.

Catherine sat in the dirt at the side of the road. Thoughts emerged slowly through the fog of hunger and fatigue. *I could bargain for as much food as I want. The sellers seemed eager. Or I can take this ball of yarn to the castle. What would the King want with a ball of yarn anyway? He might just take it and give me nothing in return. But if there is a reward . . . what if there is a reward?*

Catherine approached the castle, her hand reaching for the place where her moonstone necklace once hung. When she reached the gate, she presented the warp yarn to a royal guard and said, "I was told to bring this to the King."

The guard escorted her inside the castle and stated, "The King has decreed the sum of the reward will match the weight of the warp yarn."

He placed the ball of yarn on one side of a scale and, as it tipped, added a handful of gold coins to the other side, waiting for the scale to balance, but it did not. He added more gold coins and watched, but again the scale did not move. "There is something amiss. Call for the King!" The guard eyed Catherine warily and continued to add handfuls of coins.

Catherine saw the King, eyebrows furrowed, enter the room, and she tensed, ready to run.

The King looked at the scale and then saw Catherine. His face softened. He recognized her. She was the woman his horse knocked down in the village. He had been looking for her for since then, seeking to make amends. The King lifted the ball of warp yarn from the scale. It tipped, and gold coins fell clinking on the floor. He placed the yarn back on the scale, and the balance arm dropped.

"We think she has put an enchantment on the yarn, Sire."

The King piled more and more gold onto the scale, yet it remained motionless.

"It is curious that a ball of yarn should weigh so much," the King said with authority.

Catherine's legs began to tremble.

"But, I don't believe this woman enchanted it. My guess is that she found the ball and hoped to buy some food with it." The King took the crown off his head and placed it on the scale; the scale balanced. He laughed out loud, "What are we to make of this?" He looked at the woman standing before him. "What is your name?"

"Catherine," she whispered.

"Catherine, do you believe in destiny?" the King said thoughtfully, as he took his crown off the scale. More gold clattered to the floor as the scale adjusted. Seeing her concern, he offered a gentle, reassuring smile. "Catherine, I would like you to join me for dinner. We will sort out the payment for your kindness later." The King extended his arm and escorted Catherine to the banquet room.

Catherine shifted her weight on the elegant seat, trying to feel comfortable in such a beautiful place. She focused on the food and ate, relishing each bite. The King's voice startled her. "You are probably wondering why a ball of yarn would fetch such a handsome reward."

Catherine nodded.

"It is to finish a tapestry, a tapestry of great worth."

Catherine nodded again.

"Tell me, Catherine, how did you come to find the yarn?"

"I found it on the forest floor." She paused. "While looking for something to eat."

"Why were you looking for something to eat in the forest?"

Catherine looked at the King and saw, for the first time, his genuine interest and concern for her, and sighed. "I don't know where to begin that story."

"Excuse me a moment," the King said. Catherine sat at the table alone and waited, avoiding the confused faces of the servants waiting to clear the meal.

The King returned. "Catherine, I would like you to stay here in the castle. I have a feeling this story may take several conversations for me to hear, and you look so very tired. As curious as I am, the story will have to wait till tomorrow. My staff will show you to your room and provide you with all you need."

Catherine looked as though she might argue, but the King continued before she could refuse. "I insist you stay.

And I am the King." He smiled, and hesitantly, so did she.

Over breakfast the next morning, the King asked Catherine question after question about her story. "Tell me about where you are from. Where were you born?"

Catherine laughed, "All right, all right, but the story is a long one."

"I have time," said the King. "I want to hear it from the very beginning."

"I will tell you the story, but would you answer a question for me?"

"Of course," said the King.

"Why is the tapestry so valuable?"

"That is a longer story than you might imagine," the King said, as weariness washed over his face.

"I have time," Catherine said, smiling.

"I am the King. I can command anything to happen in this kingdom, and it will be done." His voice rang with authority. The King sighed, the authority giving way to exhaustion, then whispered, "But I cannot command death. I did not have the power to stop my wife and two children from dying. I commissioned the tapestry to be made to remember and honor them."

Catherine stared at the King who sat quietly, eyes closed. She knew that kind of love. She had seen it in her father when her mother died; she had felt it herself when her father died.

"My father had a stained glass window made to remember my mother," Catherine said gently.

Day after day, meal after meal, the two shared bits of their life through story.

The two found great comfort in each other and were married. On the night of their wedding, the King took Catherine outside the castle to the grounds below. The moon's light bathed everything in soft silver. The King held Catherine to his side. "I have a gift for you. Look up," he said simply. There, in a room just above them, was a stained glass window.

She gasped. "I've never seen a stained glass window lit up like that from the inside. It is beautiful."

"As are you."

Catherine brushed wisps of her dark hair flecked with gray from her face. "My beauty faded long ago."

"Not so," he replied.

Catherine looked into his kind face: his once-strong jaw softened with age, his dark hair streaked with gray, his eyes lined with creases made by both laughter and tears.

The King smiled. "You are like that stained glass window, my dear. Whatever beauty you had before has only been magnified by the darkness you have experienced in your life. A stained glass window sparkles when the sun is out, but when darkness comes, it can only remain beautiful if there is a light from within to illuminate it."

They stood together in silence for a moment. Then the King said, "Close your eyes." Catherine complied, and as she did, the King placed the moonstone necklace around her neck. She opened her eyes and reached for the stone as she had so many times before, and tears slipped down her cheeks.

"My moonstone," she said softly, eyes shining.

"The moon is full tonight. You could see the future," the King said, smiling.

Catherine held the King close. "My only wish for the future is to make it as happy for you as you have made it for me."

THE CRYSTAL CASTLE

When the Prince was born, the Queen cried. "His nose," she sobbed. "It looks like a banana. It's just so . . . long."

This complicated things for the King. He knew this would happen. He owed a debt to the enchantress who helped him win the heart of his wife, a debt that would show up in a horrible facial deformity. The enchantress had said, "Your Crown Prince will never marry until he admits his nose is too large."

And there it was—an ugly, banana-shaped nose on his otherwise adorable infant son.

The King didn't dare tell his wife the story of how this nose came to be. Instead, he sent for the royal scholar to procure images and accounts of great men with long noses. He sent for the royal painter to add length to the noses of all the portraits of previous sovereigns. He sent minstrels and storytellers out among the people to sing and speak of the great and varied advantages of having a large nose. He instructed young mothers to pinch and pull their babies' noses in hopes of increasing their nasal prowess. In a short time, the entire kingdom was persuaded to believe there was a wonderful and glorious history associated with long noses.

The Prince grew up being revered for the length of his nose.

When the King died, his secret died with him. The Prince and his mother cried at the gravesite of the King. The Prince required an extra-large handkerchief, proving that with a large nose, you can show grief better than the small-nosed masses.

When the Prince reached marriageable age, he and his mother watched the royal painter with his cart full of canvases and paints walk into the sunset. He was sent in search of eligible princesses whose portraits he could paint and bring back to the Prince.

A year later, twenty-nine draped easels filled the throne room. The Prince and the Queen gasped in eager anticipation as each portrait was revealed. But every portrait was the same.

The Prince looked down his long nose at each portrait. "Oh, what lovely eyes, but her nose is just too small." "What a charming smile, but her nose—you can barely see it." Soon, the last drape came down, and the Prince exclaimed, "This is it? There are no other choices?"

The Prince whined, "Mother, how can I be expected to

marry someone with such a small nose?"

"Darling, these princesses are really quite lovely. And there are twenty-nine of them. Surely there is one worthy of your affection," the Queen replied.

"Mother, you are simply not qualified to give advice on this subject. Your small nose has made you weak in judgment." The words came out with such harsh authority they left the Queen speechless. The Prince waved her away. "Leave me. Just leave. I will have to deal with this matter on my own!"

The Prince paced back and forth, looking at the portraits. "Not a single princess with superior intelligence and authority. Look at all those disgustingly tiny noses." The Prince kicked one of the velvet cloths littering the floor. Then another. He began stamping on the velvet as if it were the enemy and agonized, "I will have to remain single forever!"

He grabbed one of the velvet cloths and attempted to rip it. When it would not rip, he whapped his throne with it again and again. With his rage expired, the Prince drooped in to his throne, a cloth draped over his head, in defeat.

"I guess I'll just have to get to know them first." The Prince sighed. "Servants, bring me parchment, a pen, and the royal seal," he commanded.

The Prince spent the next year writing letters to each of the small-nosed princesses. Princess Lavender from the kingdom of Gint emerged as the favorite. In fact, she was the *only* one who wrote back after receiving letter after letter from the Prince discussing how wonderfully long his nose was.

And so it was the angelic Princess Lavender was called upon to meet the Prince.

After waiting two days for her to come, the Prince summoned his men, mounted his horse, and set out to meet the Princess; he had waited long enough. When the Prince saw the Princess's entourage, he directed his men to greet them.

The Prince approached the carriage in bold, broad steps, then knelt on one knee, bowed his head, and extended his hand for the Princess to use as she descended from the carriage.

After the Princess alighted, the Prince began to stand, but before reaching his full height, there was a great poof of violet smoke, and a malevolent laugh filled the air. Princess Lavender was suddenly encased in a small crystal castle. The Prince pressed his hands against the castle and walked around its circumference looking for any openings. When he found none he exclaimed, "What kind of evil enchantment is this?"(He would never know, for the King was no longer there to explain the curse of the enchantress.) The Prince vowed in a loud voice, "I will find a way to save you, my love."

The Princess said, "His nose can't really be that big? It must be a distortion of the crystal." But no one heard her.

The Prince was gone in a galloping gust to consult a

royal advisor. The whispers of the Princess's entourage followed him, but too slowly to make their way to his ears. "Was I mistaken, or did the Prince have a nose shaped like a banana?"

The royal advisor had no ready answer for the Prince, so he charged the Prince with a quest to find the Queen of the Fairies and ask her how to undo this enchantment.

The Prince charged off with no direction and too much determination. He traveled alone for days in search of the Fairy Queen and finally collapsed with hunger and fatigue in front of a small cottage.

A little woman, plump as a loaf of bread, came out of the door.

"Bless me, bless me, who are you? Such a sight for sore eyes. Why, I haven't seen another person for ages. Good gracious, where are my manners? You must be . . . "

"Water," the Prince whispered and fell off his horse.

"Oh dear, oh dear, oh my, my, my. What will I ever do with you? Who did you say you were again?"

The Prince pulled himself up to the gate, "Water. Food. Sleep."

"Oh, oh, oh. Come in. You look a mess. I'll get you some food to eat. Are you sick? Your nose looks swollen right off your face. Stung by a bee? My foot swelled up to the size of a watermelon once with a bee sting, but enough about me. Come in, come in. I'll get you some food and water."

The Prince gulped down the water and savored each bite of bread. The woman continued her chattering. "I've never seen a nose so large in all my days. You must be quite ill. Maybe it was an enchanted bee that stung you. It must be dreadful trying to eat and drink with such a nose—always getting in the way, tut-tut-tut. Really, it looks like a banana."

"Do you ever stop talking?" the Prince finally coughed out.

"Well, I never! At least my parents taught me some tact, young man. Don't you know it is rude to treat a hostess like that? Why, I always know when to stop talking. My parents were sticklers in teaching me the art of conversation. Passing words back and forth. Listening as much as you speak. My parents were experts. They were the Fairy King and Queen, may they rest in peace. And you, with your long nose, come in begging for food and water and sleep and then insult me for not knowing when to stop talking?! I know exactly when to stop talking—"

The Prince shifted uncomfortably, but managed an apology. "I am sorry, my good woman. I meant no offense."

"Well, your apology is accepted, mostly out of pity . . . but accepted nonetheless."

The Prince almost stomped out the door, but held his temper and managed to say, "Did you say you are a Fairy Princess?"

"I am the Queen of the Fairies now."

The Prince forgot his anger upon hearing she was the Queen of the Fairies. "You are the Queen of the Fairies? You're much bigger than I thought."

The woman gasped and her hands flew to her middle. "Well, I never!"

The Prince interjected. "What I meant was, taller. You are much taller than I thought you would be. I thought fairies were tiny and have wings."

"Oh, I see." The woman's face relaxed. "That is just how fairies are described in stories. We actually look like, well, like this," she said as she gestured to her pudgy frame.

The Prince bowed. "You, my lady, are just the person I have been in search of all these many days and nights!" The Fairy Queen blushed and giggled at his chivalry. The Prince continued, "Do you know how to rescue a princess from a crystal castle?"

"Well, if I was ever in such a predicament as that, saving a princess—or rather, in my case, a prince—I would know exactly what to do. True love is a very powerful thing. But are you quite sure the Princess wants to be rescued by someone like you? I mean, really, your nose is ridiculously large!"

"I prefer to call it a proboscis, and its size is regal. Every great thinker and ruler in my kingdom has possessed a long nose. None as long as mine, of course, for I am the Prince."

"The Prince! Well, your Royal Majesty, I hope I did not offend. I just can't seem to keep my eyes off it. It is a very large *proboscis*, my dear fellow."

The Prince touched his nose defensively, but swallowed hard and said, "Can we get back to the Princess?"

"Oh yes, the Princess. Well, like I said, it's simple. I would kiss her—or rather him, as I would be rescuing a prince instead of a princess—and that would be the end of that."

"Ha! A kiss!" The Prince smiled and was on his horse before she could say another word. "Thank you!" he called, as he rode out of sight.

The Prince approached the crystal castle with a smile teasing the corner of his lips. *A kiss. So simple.* "I have come to free you, my love!"

The Prince pressed hands, then face, with lips out-stretched, on the crystal, but his nose got in the way. He backed away surprised. He approached the crystal from a different angle, but his nose still blocked the way. Again and again he tried, but his nose always touched first.

"This can't be! My nose is regal." He tried to kiss again, but his nose was clearly in the way.

He leaned in for another kiss. It was no use. "But my nose shows my superiority. I am the Prince!" the Prince sputtered. He forced his way to the crystal once again, but made no progress.

The Prince gazed at the Princess inside the castle. *Her nose is small, but she is still lovely, and I know from our correspondence what a fine queen she'll make,* he thought.

The Prince turned his back to the crystal and let his head clunk against it. He sat there for a very long time. With some finality, he announced, "Alas, my darling, my nose seems to prevent me from rescuing you." He slumped. "My nose is just too large."

Another sudden burst of violet smoke filled the air, and when it cleared, the crystal castle was gone. There was the Princess Lavender, standing before him. He was surprised at how different she looked from her portrait. Her lips seemed much larger than he remembered.

The Princess smiled and said, "Hello."

The Prince stood, but looked away. "My love, I fear I am unworthy of your affection."

"But why?"

"The size of my nose prevents me from kissing you," the Prince said. "You are deserving of a husband you can kiss."

"The size of your nose makes you no less, or better, than me," the Princess said with authority.

The Prince looked up to see the Princess smiling. He stood, then leaned in to kiss her, but his nose bumped into her lips. The Prince groaned in frustration.

The Princess flashed an empathetic smile, then in one bold movement, positioned the Prince directly in front of her, tip-toed, and maneuvered her large lips, right past the Prince's nose, to his lips. They kissed.

"How did you manage that?" the Prince asked in awe.

"My lips have always been quite large. The royal painter portrayed them much smaller than what they were in fear you would not choose me." The Princess grinned at the Prince. "It seems, though, my large lips are absolutely perfect for you." She touched his nose.

The Prince reached for his nose, looked down, and smiled. "Indeed, they are. We shall make a fine pair."

THE HEALING STONE

"Look at this seed, Sophie. Isn't it beautiful?"

"It's so small, Papa."

"Yes, but I can still see what's inside the seed."

"What is inside the seed?" Sophie asked, squinting at the seed in Papa's hand.

"Everything it needs to become the persimmon tree it was meant to be."

"It's just a seed, Papa. How can you see so much?"

"I practice believing in things I can't see yet, but hope to see soon."

Sophie closed her eyes and scrunched her nose. Her papa laughed. "What is that face for?"

"Shhh, I'm trying to see the seed grow into a persimmon tree in my mind."

"Tell me about what you see."

Sophie puckered her lips, focusing on the images in her mind. "I see the soil. It's good soil, Papa. It's dark and warm on the top, cool underneath. The seed is inside the soil and is soaking up the water. It's swelling up, bigger and bigger, and it sprouted. Just like the little bean seeds we watched. Now the roots are growing down, and the tiny beginning of the tree is growing up. It's getting bigger and thicker, and I can see leaves and buds and flowers and, finally, fruit."

"How wonderful, Sophie! You can see something that is not there . . . yet."

Sophie opened her eyes and smiled.

"I can show you something else about this seed. This seed is special. It can predict the weather."

"It can?"

"We just have to cut it open." Papa cut the seed and showed the inside to Sophie. "What do you see?" Sophie looked perplexed. "Do you see the white in the seed?"

"Yes."

"Does the white part of the seed look like a fork, a spoon, or a knife?"

"It looks like a fork," Sophie said, surprised.

"That means it is going to be a bad winter."

"Really?"

"The persimmon seed has been accurate for as long as I can remember," said Papa.

"How did you learn so much, Papa?"

"There are seeds of knowledge floating all over the place. They just have to find a fertile mind to plant themselves in."

Sophie held a satchel of seeds to her chest. They were a parting gift from her father. She replayed the conversation in her mind again and again.

Her father had been gone for over a year now. He, like the other men in the village, had been called upon to climb the forbidden mountain to face the dragon. And he, like the other men of the village, had never returned.

When Sophie sat down to eat the afternoon meal with her grandmother, she asked her to tell the story again.

Her grandmother began, easing her aging frame into a chair.

"This mountain has always been forbidden to climb. Even before I was born, the villagers knew the mountain was cursed, and no one dared climb it. That is, until one day, when your grandfather was about your age, a man came into town and told the people about the dragon.

"The man claimed to be an expert on dragons, and he used such convincing words, the people of the village believed him. He described the dragon as a ferocious beast. As large as ten houses. As red as blood. With teeth as sharp and fierce as any sword and leather-like wings to fly. The dragon was covered in scales so thick it could not be killed, only trapped.

"'How do we trap it?!' the men exclaimed. 'We want our wives and children to be safe.'

"'The dragon wears a stone around its hideous neck. If we take the stone from it, the dragon will be trapped in stone, and you will be safe,' the man said.

"After several months of preparation, one hundred and twenty-four men followed this man up the forbidden mountain to find the dragon. Your grandfather was one of them. They carried chains and swords. They wore the thick hides of animals to protect themselves from the beast.

"Your grandfather told me how brave and clever the Dragon-catcher was. That is what they called the man, Dragon-catcher. He lured the dragon out of its dark cave and into the light of day with flattering words. 'The people of the village want to behold your greatness, to spread the story abroad of the brave dragon at the top of the mountain, who protects us.'

"All the while, there were men hidden everywhere with their chains, waiting for the dragon to emerge so they could pounce on it, then chain it down long enough for the Dragon-catcher to rip the stone from the dragon's neck.

"The dragon was so surprised, it did not even fight back. The man took the stone from around the dragon's neck and the dragon slowly began to turn to stone. Before the stone completely trapped the dragon, it dragged itself back into the cave using its powerful tail. And from inside the cave, they heard a hissing voice say, 'You fools. I can no longer protect you from the curse of this mountain.'

"'Just a guise,' the Dragon-catcher said. 'This beast would have you believe it is your protector, when in fact, it would devour your village under the right circumstances.'

"'You, who holds the stone,' the dragon's voice

whispered. 'There will be many men who will come to take it from you and return it to me. You do not know the curse you bring upon yourself for possessing it. The stone's powers were only meant for a dragon.'

"'Silence, dragon!' the Dragon-catcher called out. 'You will be silent soon. The stone will stop this nonsense.'

"'The stone's absence only has the power to take away movement from my body. It will not stop my speech, nor will it stop my fire. You are fools. But you will soon see.' The dragon's voice echoed from inside the cave.

"'Would you have this dragon freed?' the Dragon-catcher cried out.

"The men responded in a unanimous, 'No!'

"'Then trust me to be the guardian of the stone. I will take it to the top of the mountain, hide it, and guard it, so the dragon remains imprisoned, and you remain safe.'

"The men revered this Dragon-catcher and Guardian of the Stone as a hero.

"Shortly after the men came down from the forbidden mountain with their heroic tale, the valley, always so green and abundant, began to die. Over the past forty years, the ground of the village, like the dragon, slowly turned to stone. It can't produce enough to sustain us anymore." Grandma turned her gaze out the small window of their cottage. Though there was no more story to tell, it didn't feel like a proper ending, for the world outside was still grim and gray and hard.

Sophie thought of her father again. He loved to plant

seeds. It was his life's work. She loved to see the joy fill his face every time he saw something grow. For a year before he left, there were so few places left to plant, he stopped planting and started collecting. Collecting seeds from every dying plant in the village. This was the treasure she held in her hands.

Sophie closed her eyes and imagined each of the seeds growing again, each of them becoming what they were meant to become. She imagined her father coming down from the mountain, his face filled with joy, to see that his favorite seed of all had grown.

"You are my favorite seed," he always said. "An apple seed can only grow into an apple tree. A plum seed can only grow into a plum tree. But you, Sophie, you are the kind of seed that can grow into whatever you want to be."

I am going to save the village, Sophie thought to herself. *There are no men left to face the dragon, but I will face it and see what can be done to take this curse away.* This thought both startled and thrilled her.

The people of the village were talking. The men of the village were all gone. The treasures of the village had gone with them as offerings to the dragon. Nothing would grow anymore. They would have to leave.

Sophie's heart faltered at the thought of leaving. *I can't leave this place. My father is still alive. I know he is.*

Sophie prepared to take the journey up the forbidden mountain. She gathered dried food from their winter storage and hid it away in a satchel. She found a pouch and filled it with blackberry juice so she could mark the trees as she went. She knew there would be clean water to drink in the streams. She brought a knife for protection. Sophie had listened carefully to each and every story the elders had told of the forbidden mountain for a very long time. It was time to make her own story.

One night, Sophie lay awake in her bed, staring at the moon through her window. It would be only be a few days before her journey would begin. The only way to see the location of the dragon was to climb the mountain on a moonless night using the glow of the dragon's flame as a guide. It was a journey better made with company, but if anyone knew of her plan, they would stop her from going. Sophie willed sleep to come, but even when it did, her dreams were so frightening she preferred to stay awake.

The night before she left, Sophie thought of her father. She remembered a conversation they had many years ago; she was only three, or maybe four years old. She was with her father, walking toward the village when they saw a big, black bug crossing in front of them. Sophie screamed and hid behind her father, and he laughed. He laughed!

He said, "Fear is going to make that bug as big as a mountain, if you're not careful."

"It is big enough already," Sophie replied, still hiding.

"Fear is bound to make anything, including a bug, bigger than what it really is."

"I don't want it to be bigger."

"Then face it."

"Face it?"

"Touch the bug, Sophie." Then he waited. He waited and waited. She made her way slowly around his leg, reached out, and touched the bug.

"I touched the bug!"

"Was it as big as you thought?"

"No. It was much, much smaller."

"I will not make this mountain bigger than it already is," Sophie said aloud, even though there was no one to hear it. That night, Sophie began to climb.

The mountain did not to want to be climbed. Craggy rocks surrounded by loose shale made Sophie's progress difficult. It began to rain. Her torch light was soon extinguished. The rocks around her were so large she couldn't always see the light above indicating the location of the dragon's lair. She held tight to anything stable and continued. She fell so many times it felt like she hadn't made any progress at all.

Sophie kept moving through the dark, constantly checking the flickering light from the dragon's flame and marking the trail with blackberry juice. As morning approached, she stopped and carefully observed every detail of her destination, paying particular attention to how the place looked in the light. She looked for any unusual rocks or trees that would help her remember the way. Then she continued on.

Just before she reached the cave, Sophie lost her footing and fell—long and hard. A sharp rock split her leg open. Her leg throbbed, and her eyes stung with tears. She cried out, even though she knew no one could hear her. She tied the small blanket she carried around her leg, but she couldn't continue the climb. After a time, she pushed through the pain and carried on. When night finally came, she stood outside an enormous cave glowing with dragon fire.

A dragon?! What am I doing here? Exhausted, Sophie slumped to the ground and slept.

The next day, Sophie sat just outside the cave. Her leg still throbbed with pain. The blanket was soaked with her blood. She spent the day resting and preparing to face the dragon.

Finally, slowly, in the dark of night, Sophie ventured into the cave, guided by the cool, wet stone against her hands and back as she inched her way along the cave's wall.

She moved through the cave until it opened into a spacious cavern. There was a hole in the ceiling above her, so large she could see starlight. Beneath the hole was a dragon, licking a creamy white substance as it dripped from the edges of the hole. She was glad to be hidden in the shadows. She searched the cave for clues of how the dragon had treated previous guests. There were no bones or clothing laying around. There was a pile of gifts: money, jewels, and other trinkets from her village. Sophie's heart started racing. She did not have a gift for the dragon. *How could I have forgotten such an important detail?*

"I smell you," the dragon's voice rumbled. She had stopped licking and was looking around the cave.

Sophie held her breath. "Hello," she finally said, weakly.

"Ah, I thought I detected a different scent."

"Different?"

"You are not a man, but a woman. Come closer. I will not harm you."

Sophie took a few steps closer. Her entire body was shaking at the sight of this massive creature. The dragon's mouth was full of sharp teeth, just like the stories she had been told. The dragon was mostly trapped in stone, but her head and neck were free. Sophie hesitated; a mouth like that could still do so much damage. The dragon's head was spiked with horns, all very sharp. Her scaly head reminded Sophie of a very large snake, but the dragon's eyes seemed so soft and kind. Sophie tried to focus on the dragon's eyes and ignore her other ferocious features, but there were just so many of them. The dragon looked directly at her.

"You are hurt," said the dragon.

Sophie nodded.

"Dragons have the power to heal."

"They do?" Sophie asked surprised.

"Yes. Unwrap your leg and come close enough for me to lick it. When I do, your leg will be healed."

"You—you want to lick my leg?" Sophie stammered.

"I want to heal your leg, and in order to do that, I must lick it. Please trust me. I will not hurt you. I only want to help you."

Sophie listened to the dragon's tender voice; it was soft and comforting, like the sound of a lullaby. She approached the dragon and unwrapped her leg. Her whole body trembled as the dragon's huge head leaned down to lick her leg, but when the dragon's tongue touched her wound, the pain was gone. She looked at her leg; the wound was healed.

"I am not something to fear. I was once your protector," said the dragon.

"You used to protect me?"

"Are you from the village at the bottom of the mountain?"

"Yes."

"Then yes, I used to protect you and the rest of your village from the curse of the mountain."

"Is it the curse that prevents things from growing?"

"Yes."

"Can you heal the mountain like you healed my leg?"

"Yes." The dragon sighed and looked away.

"How?" Sophie asked.

The dragon looked up at the sky while she spoke. "This mountain carries the curse of stone. It is something humans do not understand, but we dragons know of things humans do not. Only a healing stone, worn by a dragon, can protect the mountain and the valley below.

"Many years ago, a man used words to flatter me, and by his cunning, he took the stone. The healing stone gives humans the ability to live forever, though it was never meant for that purpose. The man called himself the Guardian of the Stone and made his home at the top of this mountain. He wanted to live forever. I sometimes hear his voice in the wind. In order to protect the mountain and village again, I must have the healing stone. The way is difficult. The men of your village have all tried, but they have all failed."

"What happened to them?" Sophie couldn't help the interruption; her father was one of those men.

"They were turned to stone."

Sophie let out a cry. "Are they dead?"

"No."

"Is there a way to free them?" Sophie asked.

"When the healing stone hangs around my neck, all will be restored to its original state."

"They will come back to life then?"

"Yes."

"And the village soil will grow things again?"

"Yes." The dragon looked at Sophie and said, "And I will be free."

"What must I do?"

"It is a long, difficult road," the dragon said with sadness.

"There is a long, difficult road behind me, too." Sophie smiled. "What do you know of the journey ahead?"

"The stones speak."

"What do they say?"

"They will say anything to stop you from making the journey. They will convince you to turn around, and if you listen—if you turn back—you will be turned to stone. These voices are powerful. The only person who has resisted them is the man who stole the stone."

"How do you think he did it?"

"When he took the healing stone from me, the curse of the mountain was unleashed. I believe the stones were eager to let him pass, for he unwittingly released their powers."

Sophie was quiet now.

"If you make it past the stones, you must find the man and convince him to give the healing stone back to me."

"I must try."

"Then wait until you are rested and have the light of the sun to guide you. You may spend the night here. I do not have much to offer you but warmth and a little moon milk."

"Is that what you were drinking when I came in?" Sophie's face brightened.

"Yes."

"I would very much like to try it."

"Take a goblet from the pile of treasures and collect the milk in it."

Sophie wrapped herself in a blanket she found among the treasures and waited as the cup filled, drip by drip.

When there was enough to drink, she lifted the cup to her lips. She smiled in delight with her first taste of moon milk. The liquid was sweet on her tongue and seemed to fill her with light.

"It is very satisfying, isn't it?" said the dragon.

"Yes." She placed the cup out again to collect more. "Thank you for sharing it with me."

The next morning, Sophie stood to continue the journey, strengthened and whole.

The Dragon looked at the young woman leaving the cave and called out, "Don't turn back, no matter what the stones say."

"I won't."

Sophie looked for the best place to start her ascent. Twenty feet up the path, she saw a stone statue of a man fallen to the ground, looking up, his face in anguish. Sophie stopped. *Maybe I should turn back*, she thought.

"Yes, turn back. Turn back now. You are too young to make this journey."

The voices came from everywhere.

"If you turn back now, you can still live and return to your people," the voices said soothingly. "You do not have to risk being turned into stone. Someone older and stronger was meant for this journey."

Sophie took a few steps up the path.

"Turn around. You will never make it. Turn back now while you still can. You have no chance of success. If you turn around and leave this place, you can still live. One step further, and you will surely die."

"I will not die, but be turned to stone," Sophie said aloud.

"And do you think someone will save you? Do you really think someone will ever be brave enough to get past us? Look around you. Look up the path. Look at how many men have tried and failed. The mountain is made of men who have been turned to stone. But you are a girl, and still quite young, so we'll let you turn back now without any consequences."

Sophie stared at the path before her. Stone statues of men lined it, each with a look of torment on his face. She continued.

"Turn back! What do you think you can accomplish, anyway? Do you really think the dragon will change everything when you bring back the healing stone? The dragon will eat you! You think these men can be flesh again? The dragon only told you that to convince you to go. The dragon wants freedom . . . and a tasty snack." The voices laughed.

Sophie began to doubt. *Maybe the dragon is using me. What if my father can't be restored?*

"The dragon *is* using you and will eat you. And your father will always be made of stone. You cannot succeed. Turn around now, and we will not turn you into stone."

The voices were powerful in her mind. They pounded against her courage, and she felt so very tired. *Maybe I could just rest a little.*

"Rest, yes, rest. Turn around and try again another day. Wait until you are stronger."

A thick, white mist settled on the path around Sophie. She couldn't remember why she was there. She felt so tired. *I want to go home.* Sophie couldn't see the many men trapped in stone reminding her of what would happen if she turned back now. *What was it the dragon said?* She stopped and held her head, trying to lift the foggy feeling from her mind. The voices were so insistent. Sophie put a finger in her ears to stop the noise. The haze began to lift. She could see the path again and continued, faster than before. She knew the voices were still there, but with her fingers in her ears, they were muffled and no longer had the same power over her. *I can finish this journey.*

She continued on. The stone men with stories of fear etched in their faces were sparse now. When the last of these men were lost behind her, the mountain opened up into a beautiful green meadow with fruit trees and wildflowers. Sophie was so astonished she fell to the ground.

She could see a crumpled old man sitting at the base of a plum tree. Sophie couldn't tell if the man was alive or dead. She unplugged one ear. The voices were gone. She unplugged the other ear and approached the man. He didn't take any notice of her. His head hung low to the ground; she couldn't see his face, only thin, white hair moving in the breeze.

"Hello," she said.

The man tried to lift his head, but couldn't. A wheezy whisper escaped him, "Food."

Sophie picked two plums and sat down. She handed one to the man. "Here is a plum."

The man ate it with much more speed than she thought he was capable of. She handed him the other plum. He devoured it. Sophie stood, then picked and dropped plum after plum at the man's feet. He ate them all. He turned his head to the side to see her. "Take it," he wheezed. "Take it."

"Take what?" said Sophie confused. "The plums?"

"No, the stone. The healing stone. It is hanging around my neck."

"Oh."

"Take it!" he snapped. "I cannot bear to live like this any longer! I am always hungry, but my body is too old to gather food. I cannot die from the hunger, but can't you see? I cannot live either! Take the stone and its curse with you. I want nothing of it."

Sophie looked at the man, still confused.

"Take it!" he snapped again. Sophie jumped, then leaned down to remove the stone from the old man's neck. When she did, he sighed and leaned his head against the plum tree. Relief replaced the misery in his face, and he was gone.

Sophie placed the stone in her satchel and ran across the meadow. She plugged her ears once again and made her way down the mountain to the dragon's cave.

"I have the stone!" Sophie called out. "I have it!" Sophie

stumbled into the cave breathless. "I did it. I got the stone."

The dragon's look of surprise made Sophie laugh.

"Hang it from my neck," the dragon said.

Sophie looked at the healing stone. It was smooth and a translucent yellow. Around the stone was a casing with a cord so it could be worn like a necklace. But it was much too small for the dragon's neck.

"How?" It came out in a disappointed sob. "This cord is too small." Sophie sat down hard and put her face in her hands.

"You've come so far." The dragon gently nudged Sophie's back with her nose. "I'm sure there is a way to hang it from my neck."

"There is no twine or rope here. Just rocks and trees," Sophie cried. The dragon listened. Sophie's tears came from a much deeper place than a simple lack of rope. "I am too tired to go to the village and get rope. No one even knows I've gone. Well, they do know now, but they probably won't let me come back. They'll send someone else to do the job I started but can't finish."

"It doesn't have to be a rope," the dragon said softly.

Sophie's sobs stopped, and she laughed at the simple solution. "Of course!"

She stood up, took off her underskirt, and ripped it into strips. She tied the strips together and slipped them through the stone's casing. She climbed the dragon's stony back, then the brilliant red scales of her neck. After maneuvering around the dragon's horns, she tied the ends of the cloth together and the stone hung from the dragon's neck. Sophie held on tight as the dragon shook off the crumbling stone, scrambled out of the cave, and launched into the air. Sophie yelped, and the dragon laughed.

"I can put you down if you would like."

Sophie looked at the mountain below and took a long glorious breath. "No, not yet. I like flying."

The dragon flew, wings beating the air. Sophie stared in wonder at the world from the sky. She felt the wind in her face and the freedom of flight.

"The mountain is so beautiful from up here," Sophie sighed.

She noticed movement on the mountain, a lot of it, and exclaimed, "My father! My father and the other men! They are free. Please take me down."

The dragon swooped down and landed on the path by men shaking stone from their bodies.

"Papa?" Sophie called out. "Papa?" She made her way along the path. "Papa?" Each face looked at her in curiosity as she ran from man to man looking for her father. Finally, she saw him. "Papa!" She ran to him, and they embraced.

"Sophie, what are you doing here?" he asked, astonished.

"I came to free you."

"How did you make it past the cursed stone voices?"

"I plugged my ears, Papa."

He laughed, "Why didn't I think of that?"

"I thought of seeds, Papa. I thought how they need a fertile piece of ground to grow. The words of the stones were like seeds; I knew they would take root unless I stopped them somehow. I plugged my ears so they couldn't grow."

"How very wise." Her father smiled. "You have grown into someone even more wonderful than I imagined."

"Thank you, Papa." She held him tight.

When the men were free from stone, they gathered around Sophie and the dragon to hear the story of their freedom.

The men cheered, and each one thanked Sophie and the dragon before they made their way down the mountain.

When Sophie and her father descended from the mountain into the village, what they saw made them stop. It was as if the trees, the plants, the flowers, the very ground, had also shaken off the stone curse. Everything was green and alive.

Sophie's father wrapped his arms around his daughter and smiled. Sophie held the satchel of seeds he had given her and grinned, "Let's plant some seeds."

THE CRANE'S GIFT

The evening sky was a peaceful orange reflected on the lake. A long-legged crane dipped her beak in and out of the water with fluid grace. Her feathers shone soft white against the colored sky. The crane's round floating nest, with her treasure of eggs, was some distance from her now. She continued stepping through the water in search of food. She did not see the net.

Water churned around her as she pecked at the net, tangled and barbed, with her beak. Feathers flapping, beating the water hard, splashing with reckless movements, she fought against the net, but she could not free herself. In fact, she had only entangled herself more.

She was down on one knee, thrashing, wild-eyed, and disheveled, when a young man saw her. He approached the graceful bird as gently as a flower blooms. The man stood close enough to touch the crane, but remained still. She thrashed, squawked, and hopped back, away from the man, then flopped into the water. With powerful wings beating, she stood up and looked at the man, beak bared.

In a slow, careful movement the man held out his hand, palm up. His breathing was long and deep. His eyes stared at the water. He did not speak but communicated his intention through his gesture: *I'm just here to help.*

The crane was still. She observed the man with her sharp eyes. Finally, she hopped awkwardly toward the man until she was close enough to touch him and stopped. For some time, she stood waiting, then, in a sudden, graceful movement, she placed her beak in the man's outstretched hand.

She flinched when she saw the blade of the knife come from the man's pocket, but she did not thrash; she was in his hands now.

When the man finished the slow, deliberate work of releasing the bird from bondage, the moonlight looked like liquid silver on the water. The man made his way to the shore. The crane made her way to her nest. The man slept, and the crane cared for her eggs.

When the first pink light of morning touched the horizon it kissed the lake, and the lake blushed. The crane walked toward the man sleeping on the shore. As she walked, her long, thin bird legs grew heavy with flesh. Her soft, white feathers wove themselves into a thin, white cloth. Her graceful neck held a head of long, black hair and an angelic face. The crane transformed into a woman who watched the man as he slept.

When he finally awoke, there was fruit laid out before him. He startled at the sight. He looked up to see who his benefactor was and startled again. The woman before him was exquisite. He drank in her beauty with a thirst he didn't know he had.

"I thought you might be hungry," she said softly. "I saw your long, gentle work with the crane last night."

The man hopped up, searching for the crane, but when he could not see it, he settled back down, assuming the bird had flown away with its newfound freedom.

"Thank you for the food." The man smiled and offered her some.

They ate and talked all through the day, and when the sky told them night was near, they promised to meet again the next morning.

With the mask of night, the woman touched the water and became a crane once again. She searched out her nest, her babies. She cared for them, but when morning approached, she transformed into a woman once again. She gathered fruit and met the young man on the shore where they had conversed the day before. The day seemed short with such good company, and again, they promised to meet the next day.

This is how the days and nights continued until the baby cranes were old enough to face the world alone; the woman and man were wrapped in love, then wed.

A few blissful years passed before the strain of meager resources penetrated the young man's mind and robbed him of peace. "You deserve so much more than I can give you." It came out in a burst of anger, but hidden behind the anger was the deep sadness he felt. "I will leave you and search for better work."

"Don't leave. Stay with me. I have all I need," she said in her soft, calm voice.

But the man was intent on his wanting and prepared to leave the next morning.

That night, as the man slept, his wife made her way to the lake. When she touched the moonlit water, she was a crane once again. All through the night, she pulled and pecked at feathers until her bird body was bloody and bruised. The white feathers lay on the ground all around her. When morning crept slowly into the valley, she left the water and became a woman again. Her eyes were dull and tired. Her skin was bruised, her hair thin and tangled, but her feathers had become an exquisite white cloth. She wrapped her tender flesh in a brown dress she had brought from home, then picked up the beautiful white cloth. She took it home as a gift for her husband.

"What happened to you?" The man looked at his wife in alarm.

"It is nothing. Look, look at what I have made for you to sell. Take this cloth to the market without naming a price, and you will come back with all you desire."

The man did as he was told.

The market was noisy and crammed with people: coins clinking, voices haggling, men bumping into each other for better purchasing position. The young man sighed and unwrapped the cloth he carried. The moment he shook the cloth in the sunlight, the noise stopped. It was as if the cloth carried the enchantment of the moon with its soft, silvery glow. Potential buyers approached the cloth in reverence.

"This is worth three hundred gold pieces," a buyer announced.

"Three hundred?" A buyer called out incredulously. "I would pay six hundred!"

"I have a thousand gold pieces I can offer you right now," said a man, pulling at the bag of coins on his belt.

And so it went, until the young man carried home as much money in one day as he had earned in the last five years.

"We are rich! You will not believe how much that cloth sold for." He picked up his wife and held her tight. She winced at the pain but smiled at her husband's happiness.

They lived for a few years in comfort, but money dissipates over time and want fills the space. Discontentment spilled out in words of determination: "I will go to the city and make enough money to provide all you could ever want."

"I have all I want," she replied, but her words fell to the ground like leaves in autumn.

And so, that night, while her husband slept, the woman approached the lake once again and began the painful, bloody work of plucking feathers.

The next morning, the man found his wife sprawled in a chair. Her hair was in tangles, her skin was yellow-green and sagging. The absence of her once-sweet beauty left him with a bitter aftertaste.

"Why are you sleeping on the chair? Am I not an acceptable sleeping companion?" The words spat from his mouth.

"I am sorry. I worked all through the night to make this for you. By the time I got home, I was too tired to come into bed. But here, see, I made you more cloth to sell at the market."

His face brightened. "This will fetch a large sum at the market! It is even more beautiful than the last. I will bring you home a treasure for your work."

"You are my treasure, husband. *You* are my treasure." But the words, like dust settling on flat surfaces, went unnoticed.

Later that evening, the man burst through the door, "The cloth sold for two thousand gold coins! There are three others who would buy it for the same price tomorrow. Can you make more?"

His wife was slumped at the table, but smiled and nodded.

Again, she approached the water by moonlight. Again, she transformed, then plucked and pulled out each feather. This time, she forced her tired body all the way to the bed to sleep by her husband. Little spots of blood stained the blanket.

In the morning, the man stared at his wife while she slept. She looked old. Old and used up. He shuddered. Full of disgust, he woke her with his impatient words. "There is only one cloth. I need three! There are three willing to buy. Why did you not make three?"

"I only have time to weave one cloth each night," she said, shaking sleep from her mind.

"I will help you weave the other two. Come let us work."

"This is something you cannot help me with. It is a work I must do alone."

"Surely, I can help you. I have willing buyers," the husband insisted.

"They must wait, my love."

"Can't you weave more now?"

"No, it can only be done by the light of the moon," she said in a resolute tone.

"I will help you tonight then."

"No." She burst into tears. "Please don't try to help me. You must never see me weave the cloth."

That night, when the woman heard the long, deep breaths of her husband sleeping beside her, she made her way toward the lake. But her husband was not asleep. He would assist his wife. They would weave two cloths together tonight and make his buyers happy.

The man followed his wife quietly and watched for the perfect moment to offer his assistance. He held in a gasp as he watched his wife touch the water and turn into a crane. His mind was still reeling with this enchantment, when, in horror, he witnessed each violent, jerky movement as she plucked and pulled out all of her feathers. The man held his stomach as he watched. When the work was done, he saw the feathers transform into the cloth. He made his way home in swift silence so she would not know he had seen her.

When his wife walked through the door, she collapsed. Her body carried a strong tint of purple and blue. Her hair was thin, her face tired and sunken. He stopped and stared at her. Tears stung his eyes. To him, she had never looked more beautiful. He lifted her with the same tenderness he felt the first time they met, and laid her on the bed.

"Dear wife, rest."

"The cloth. Did you get the cloth?" she asked sleepily.

"Yes, thank you. There will be no more need for weaving, my love."

"But there is one more buyer," she said, grabbing his hand.

"Perhaps, but I am not willing to sell."

"But why?" she questioned.

"I did not realize until now: I already have all the treasure I need."

FETCH ME A STAR

There once was a knight with a brave and gentle heart tucked inside a tall, awkward body. It was hard to say if his armor was a little too wide and short, or if his arms and legs were a little too long and thin. But it was plain to see he was all arms and legs . . . and hair. His hair was bright red and unruly, and, of course, he was not without freckles.

The Knight had eyes for only one thing—and she was a beauty, with sapphire eyes and a dazzling smile. In real life, he didn't dare approach her, but in his dreams he talked with her every night.

Once in a while, dreams become reality, and reality becomes what we dream. And so it was on one autumn day, in the castle garden, the Knight stammered out his affection for the Princess in person. "Y-y-you are as beautiful as the stars."

She could barely stifle a smirk, "Who are you?"

His knight heart was pounding, but his lips wouldn't move.

"I'm waiting for an answer," she huffed in annoyance.

"Can't think," he whispered.

"Your name is 'Can't Think'?" she said with one eyebrow raised.

"No, uh . . . uh . . . it's Henry," he said, relieved his name finally came to his mind.

"Well, Harold, if you want to have any hope of courting me, you must bring me a . . . " She took some time to think, but the Knight was willing to wait. He would bring anything to have the hope of courting this beautiful creature.

"A star! Right out of the night sky. That should keep you out of my—I mean, that would be a noble gesture to prove your love. If you can do that, I might let you talk to me."

The Knight nodded with enthusiasm, smiled, and left.

Later that evening, the Knight let his desire to procure a star guide his feet. (It guided his feet because he didn't have a horse.)

The Knight climbed to the top of the tallest mountain he could find, lifted his long arms to the sky, and began snatching at stars. He jumped and lunged at stars all through the night until the stars began to fade into the morning sky. He would just have to wait for nighttime to try again. While making his way back down the mountain, the Knight inadvertently walked into a dark circle of grass beneath a tree. It was a fairy ring! The Knight instantly became very small and was transported into the center of a fairy gala. There was music and dancing, tables of food and drink, and glittering fairies standing about him everywhere.

The Knight found himself at a table with several giggling fairies. "Oooh, it's a knight!"

"Perhaps he's on a quest," said a fairy with blue hair and big eyes.

"Oh, quests make such great stories," said a fairy whose silver hair shimmered like jewelry.

The Knight cleared his throat and said, "I am on a quest for true love."

With this, the fairies began bobbing up and down, bumping into each other with their tittering. "True love?!"

"My love is like a star with golden hair and sparkling eyes."

"Oooh," the fairies exclaimed. The Knight had their full attention now, but he didn't know what to do with it, so he remained silent. Without warning, the fairies all began banging their forks and spoons on the table chanting, "What's the quest! What's the quest! What's the quest?"

"I must pluck a star directly from the sky and present it to the Princess to prove my love."

The whispers flashed around the table, just soft enough that the Knight had to strain to hear them.

"That's impossible."

"She must not love him in return."

"Probably told him that to get rid of him."

The fairies looked at the Knight and smiled sweetly, "The Fairy Queen could help you with your quest."

"Where is the Fairy Queen?"

"She's over there." The fairies all pointed to a beautiful fairy surrounded by a group of other beautiful fairies standing by the punch bowl—they were all giggling.

The Knight made his way across the dance floor, head down, muttering to himself. "Why do they always have to travel in packs? It's hard enough to talk to one, but a whole group? And the giggling, oh, the giggling. If only I could get her alone, I might be able to remember what I need to say."

The giggling suddenly got louder, and he looked up; they were all staring at him. He wanted to hide inside his armor, but since he couldn't, he blushed.

"His face is as red as his hair!" More giggling.

He said, "Punch."

They giggled, handed him some punch, and waited to see if he would say more.

"It's good. Punch."

"Would you like some more?" It came as a chorus.

"Is one of you the Fairy Queen?" It surprised them all how many words came out of his mouth at the same time.

"Oooh, the Fairy Queen, you want to talk to the Fairy Queen . . ."

The Fairy Queen waved them all away and touched the Knight on the arm. "I am the Fairy Queen. What do you need, Brave Knight?"

"A star. I'd like to take a star from the sky and give it to my one true love as a token of my affection, but I am not sure how to get one."

"A noble quest, indeed." The Fairy Queen nodded with approval. "You must take Two Feet to Four Feet, who will guide you to No Feet. No Feet will take you to the stairs without steps, and there, you will find your star."

The Knight smiled weakly and thought, *Why can't girls just say what they mean?*

Suddenly, something thumped the Knight on the head. It was an apple. Startled, the Knight looked around and now found himself leaning against an apple tree. A horse was grazing in a nearby meadow. "Was I dreaming? Take Two Feet to Four Feet? What does that mean?" he said to himself in a daze.

"Stand up and walk toward me," the horse replied.

"You talk?"

"Occasionally," said the horse.

"All right then. If I'm Two Feet and you're Four Feet, I need you to take me to No Feet. Do you know what that means?"

"Of course," said the horse.

"Wonderful, because I had absolutely no idea." The Knight hopped on the horse, who galloped down the mountain side.

The horse slowed to a trot when he reached a lake. "In there, you'll find No Feet."

"A fish?"

"That's my best guess," said the horse.

"Will the fish talk, too?"

"I hope so."

The Knight dismounted then bowed his head. "Thank you for your kindness."

The horse whinnied and galloped away.

The Knight, unsure how to attract a fish's attention, stood at the edge of the lake, studying the light dancing on the ripples of water. "This is awkward," he muttered to himself.

"Not as awkward as talking with gills," the fish said, bobbing in the water just below the Knight's gaze.

The Knight jumped, then smiled at the large, gray-green fish looking up at him and bowed. "Thank you for conversing with me even at such a great cost of awkwardness."

"Sure. No problem."

"Are you the fish that knows the way to the stairs without steps?"

"The very one," said the fish.

"Would you take me to these famed stairs without steps so I can fetch a star for my true love?"

"Jump in and hold onto my tail."

The Knight jumped in the water and grabbed hold of the fish's tail. The fish swam with great speed, whipping the Knight back and forth the entire way. When the fish finally stopped, the Knight was sick to his stomach, and his armor was full of water. The Knight looked up to behold the brightest, most distinct rainbow he had ever seen. "The stairs without steps?" he whispered.

"You guessed it." And the fish was gone.

"How do I climb that?" the Knight wondered aloud, but this time, there was no talking beast to help him.

He tried to lift his legs onto the violet band of the rainbow, but as long as his legs were, they couldn't quite reach. He laid down on his belly at the end of the rainbow and tried to crawl up it like a baby. In a full suit of armor, this looked laughable and was completely ineffective. Finally, he grabbed hold of the red band with his left hand and the violet band with his right hand and pulled himself up, hand over hand. Progress was slow, but the Knight finally reached the top. He carefully placed one foot on the yellow band and the other on the green band and pulled himself up to his full height. He was too busy looking down to look up and see the stars. Quite a natural response, really, as the rainbow didn't look like it would bear much weight. The Knight's heart was beating fast, and his palms were sweaty from the exertion.

The Knight looked up and there, just above his head, was a star. A beautiful star. The most beautiful star he had ever seen, partly because it was glittering and silvery, and partly because it was close enough to reach. The Knight lifted his long arms, grasped the star on either side, and yanked, but the star did not move. He tugged harder, but nothing happened. Forgetting his apprehension of balancing on a rainbow, the Knight took a running jump and grabbed the star, pulling it with all his might, but the star didn't budge. There he was, hanging from a star, with long legs dangling out of his armor and red hair flopping back and forth in the breeze.

He tried hoisting himself up on the star in an effort to weigh it down, but, as you can imagine, that didn't end well. The Knight went toppling down, bounced off the rainbow, and slid backwards down the colored bands on his shiny armor-encased behind. He closed his eyes, braced for impact, and hit the ground with a loud THUMP.

When he opened his eyes, he was indoors. He was in his sleeping quarters, on the floor. He had just fallen out of bed.

"Was that all a dream?" he asked in wonder.

No one responded.

The next day, the Knight made his way to the castle garden. He needed to see the Princess again and was summoning the courage to ask her for a different quest. He stood behind the trees and listened as a young man played his lute and sang a love song to the Princess.

Before the Knight could even worry about his competition, the Princess spoke. "That was supposed to be a love song? It sounded like cats fighting. If you want to prove your love to me, you'll have to do better than that. Much better. In fact, don't bother coming back. And, I would seriously consider never opening your mouth to sing again."

Her words came out so quick and sharp the Knight felt

to grab his sword to parry them.

The Knight peeked through the trees and took a good, long look at his "love." Her eyes were still a dazzling sapphire, but they held no kindness. Her lips were still an irresistible shade of pink, but they were neither soft nor inviting.

The Knight took in a deep breath, smiled, and walked away. He was no longer in need of courage to seek a different quest to "prove his love." In fact, he felt braver than he ever had before. Brave enough to search for the kind of love you could feel as well as see.

THE RELUCTANT KNIGHT

There once was a princess with bright, inquisitive eyes and ideas to share.

She was surrounded by brothers: three older and two younger. She watched them train for battle every day. They practiced sword skills. They ran, jumped, climbed, and maneuvered on horses. They planned strategies with small, rough-carved, wooden men, under the direction of her father.

Then, one day, she made a suggestion. "What if you put the bulk of the army over here?" She pointed at the map. "Then you could cut off the supply route to the kingdom. Soldiers can't last long without food."

"That's ludicrous. Why aren't you doing embroidery or something?" her oldest brother retorted.

"Don't you have a ball gown to try on?" another brother sneered.

"You're a princess. Princesses aren't brave or smart— they're pretty." The brothers dismissed her.

The Princess's face turned red in her passion. "What is the use of being pretty if you can't do anything?!"

"Princesses don't need to *do* anything, darling," said her father.

The Princess stomped her foot and whirled around to leave in a rage, but her father only smiled; she looked so adorable when she was mad.

The Princess spent her days watching her father and brothers from afar, wishing they would listen to her. She was smart and brave . . . and angry. *Why should being a girl make you any less important?*

One day, she threw a fit when her brothers teased her. She took off her shoe and threw it so hard it made a hole in the door when it collided.

"Princesses do not throw things. What do you have to be so angry about, anyway?" her father scolded and sent her to her room.

The Princess fumed but said nothing. That night, she found a small suit of armor and a sword and hid them in her quarters. She made a dummy out of one of her dress forms, using bed clothing and blankets. *If princesses can't be angry, then I'll pretend to be a knight.* She released her anger on the dummy, slicing it with a sword and hitting it with her fists. At first, her dainty little hands were bruised and swollen, but she got stronger each night.

While no one was looking, she snuck into the room

where battle strategy was taught and rearranged her brother's battle plans. Her father would complement the strategies, unaware it was his daughter's genius he admired.

A year passed, and tension filled the castle. The five princes walked with stiffness, heads bowed. The kingdom was under attack. The King had been captured. The princes would leave for battle the next morning.

A week passed with no word from the King or the princes. The knights were fatigued and without leadership. It was only a matter of days before the castle would fall.

The Princess walked into a room strewn with maps, diagrams, and many young men wearing defeat on their faces. Her elegant gown, a soft blue, juxtaposed against the sharp dark grey of armor and swords.

She listened to the knights proposing battle strategies; she studied their plans carefully and could see their recommendations would be ineffective. She wondered, if she suggested a change of strategy as herself, would they accept it? She already knew the answer. *Princesses do not know anything about battle strategies. Proper etiquette and fine clothing, of course, but not battle strategies.* Her fists clenched, and she spun out of the room. *Most princesses don't know anything about battle strategy, but I do, and I am not going to let my kingdom fall just because I happen to be a girl.*

She took the scissors from her embroidery kit and cut her hair. She took dirt and rubbed it across her brow, then smeared it on her cheeks, chin, and hair. She pricked her finger with her embroidery needle and applied the blood on her chin and forehead. She pulled the linen hood over her head and put on the suit of armor she practiced with nightly.

She looked at herself in the mirror and cringed; she looked like her brothers. *I don't want to be a man. I like being a woman.* She grabbed her sword and helmet and thought fast about how she could inspire the loyalty and trust of these men. They wouldn't recognize her. She was taking a risk, but she could see their minds were in chaos; they had little hope and even less leadership. They just might follow any knight who had a plan, especially a plan that could work.

The Princess ran from her quarters to the battle room, she entered the room breathless and announced in her deepest, commanding voice, "I've just returned from the battle. I have a plan I think will work."

The knights stopped what they were doing and looked at the knight before them. An awkward silence filled the room, then one of the knights sitting at the table put his fist down hard and said, "If you have a plan, say it!"

The Princess now knew they believed she was a knight and began. She grabbed the wooden pieces representing men. "The bulk of their force is stationed here. If we send a small group of our men to attack here—"

"It will be slaughter!"

The Princess straightened, "Not if we only pretend we

will fight. When our men see the numbers of the opposing forces, they need to retreat into the woods here, but they will only act like cowards. What they are actually doing is drawing the army away from the castle and into the woods. The commanders of the opposing army will think they can squash such a small army with very little effort, so they will follow our men into the woods. Our army will stay far enough ahead of them that they cannot engage us in battle. Then we will surprise them."

"We surprise them? With what?!"

"We hide the largest army we can muster in the woods. It will have to be done with the cover of night. Their army will march right past our men hidden in the woods. When the last of their army has entered the woods, we surround them and attack from every side. They will be so disoriented we have a chance of victory, even though they have the larger army."

One knight exclaimed, "I think this could work." The other knights nodded their heads in agreement.

"I plan to take whatever men will join me to rescue the King while this battle is taking place."

"I will join you," several men called out.

"Now, let's put this plan into action!" She pounded her fist on the table.

The knights exclaimed, "Huzzah!"

Assignments were made, and the Princess found herself leading a small group of knights to the castle where her father was held captive.

On the battlefield, the plan was presented to the five princes. They each rallied their men in support. That night, the Princess experienced the clank of swords, the power of silencing foes, the thrill of stealth and intrigue. And success. She found the King and brought him safely home. The battle in the woods was fierce, but her strategy led them to victory. The opposing forces surrendered, and their king made a treaty promising peace after seeing his much larger army was no match for the cunning of this kingdom.

The Princess knew she held the respect of all the knights in her kingdom. She was proud of her success. Her father was home, her brothers were safe, and her kingdom was no longer being threatened. Everything happened exactly as she hoped.

The whispers were already traveling through the ranks that the King planned to appoint this brave and loyal knight as his head strategic advisor. But . . . that wasn't what she really wanted. She could see being a man didn't honor her; it felt instead like an empty substitute.

She did want respect. She knew she was as brave and smart as any knight in the kingdom, but because she was a woman, no one expected that of her. *But what is the cost for respect? Is there another way?*

The next day, the King called for a ceremony to honor the heroic knight who had saved the kingdom.

The Princess bathed, then put on her full armor, but the weight in her heart made every movement feel heavy.

She walked through the long line of knights. They pounded the stone floor of the castle with flag poles in a rhythmic pattern. "Huzzahs" filled the air as she stood before the King. The King hushed the crowd.

"Remove your helmet and state your name," the King commanded.

The Princess lifted the helmet from her head and smiled at her father. "I think you know my name."

"It—it was you?" the King managed to stammer as he took a step back.

Several knights dropped the flags they held; the wooden poles clattered on the floor. Some took off their helmets to see more clearly. Her brothers stood with their mouths open.

"It was me," said the Princess.

"But . . ."

"But, what? Just because I am a Princess doesn't mean I can't be brave, or smart, or willing to do whatever it takes to save our kingdom."

"Obviously . . ." The King paused, thinking through his next move. "You are as good as any man in my kingdom, and I would like to make you a knight. I would also like to offer you the esteemed position of head battle strategist for your cunning and brave plan that saved," he paused again, "our kingdom."

"With a noble heart, I must refuse this offer as it stands."

The King was utterly perplexed now. "Why?"

The Princess faced her brothers, then the crowd.

"I know I am as brave and valuable as any of you."

The knights, recovered from the shock, filled the air with more "Huzzahs!" and beat their poles on the ground.

The Princess silenced the men with a gesture. "I do not want to be a knight. I like being a Princess, but I want you to listen to me just as I am."

The castle was silent.

The King looked at his lovely daughter and let out a long, loud "Huzzah!" The knights joined him and added the rhythmic beat of wooden poles.

And so it was, in this kingdom, a Princess brought power, glory, and respect to all women by choosing to be exactly what she was.

BEAUTY'S CURSE

When the Princess squalled her first, thin newborn cry, the King let go of the breath he had held long and deep. The labor was long and complicated, and the Queen did not survive. The King burst through the door to the shock of his beloved wife gone and then a bigger shock. The Princess did not look like any of the other girls the kingdom.

Her head was wrinkled and misshapen, her lips pulled far to one side; she had small piggy eyes, large flapping ears, and hair sprouting out in all directions.

He did what any good king would do—what any good father would do. He banned mirrors from the kingdom. There they were, a huge pile of gold and glass, lying just outside the kingdom with a sign posted that read, "Beauty is Bigger than a Reflection Here."

The King decreed to all his subjects, "We will be the best and only reflection the Princess has of her beauty."

And so, the Princess grew up in a kingdom where no one knew what they looked like. Beauty showed itself in laughter, in kindness, in friendship, in love, instead of a reflection.

In the dark of night, the King and Princess sat in the castle tower looking at the stars. The Princess would connect the brightest of the stars to make pictures, and the King would tell her stories to match the pictures.

"When I grow up, I want to be just like you." The Princess grinned up at her father.

"Then you'll have to practice doing the things I do. It is your turn to make a story from the stars."

The Princess laughed and told a story of a mouse king who saved the kingdom from cats.

In the light of morning, the King and Princess traveled the many roads of their kingdom in an open carriage. When the King saw a squabble among neighbors, a child without shoes, or a mother carrying more than one child, he would stop the carriage and hop out to assist.

One day, the Princess noticed an old woman carrying a heavy load on her back. She stopped the carriage, hopped out, and offered to carry the woman's load before the King even noticed the woman. The King smiled at his daughter and said, "I've never seen anything more beautiful in my life."

And so it was, the Princess's unique beauty was felt in every part of the land, and no one questioned it.

The King nearly forgot to feel anxious when his daughter reached marriageable age. The realization hit him like a surprise javelin. How would he preserve her sense of beauty in the face of princes who didn't know any better?

The royal lace maker was called. Her old, bony fingers tatted white threads into beautiful, intricate patterns. A veil that covered her from head to foot was presented to the Princess on the day of her first royal suitor.

The first prince was dashing and had all kinds of charming words to say. For many days, he was enamored with the Princess's wit and charm. Enamored, that is, until she took off the veil of lace. He had been through rather rigorous training in charm and did not let the slightest bit of the horror he felt at her appearance, show on his face. The following day, he left.

The Princess questioned her father, "Why did he leave?"

The King replied, "You are so beautiful, my love, he must have felt unworthy to be your husband."

The next prince came, sword in hand, his strength both obvious and obnoxious. The Princess captivated him from the moment they started talking. He was instantly fascinated by her ideas on ruling a kingdom and completely astonished at how she and her father went into their kingdom, offering assistance to those in need. But, alas, when she removed her veil, he too left the kingdom without a word.

"Why? Why did he leave? Why do they leave after they see me?"

"My darling, it is because they feel unworthy of your beauty."

Prince after prince came and courted, and prince after prince left without a word.

After several years of courting with no proposals, the Princess spoke the words of her heart.

"Now I see that it is as much a curse to be beautiful as it is to be very ugly. Both get in the way of loving and being loved."

The King never spoke the words of his heart, but felt them keenly day after disappointing day. It was his deepest wish that his daughter could love and be loved by a husband.

So many suitors had come to the kingdom interested, but left repulsed. Would any suitor be able to see his daughter's beauty as clearly as he could?

Sometime during this mess of courtship, there came an old traveling minstrel whose songs and stories delighted the villagers to distraction.

The King decided a distraction was just what they needed and sent an invitation for the minstrel to entertain them at the royal palace.

The Princess sat on her throne, unveiled. This was not a suitor, after all, but a promising performance.

The minstrel arrived, bowed, and spun his spell in music and words.

The Princess's clear and joyful laugh filled the throne room. The King's belly laugh was loud and long—as a king's laugh should be.

The Princess lost herself in the revelry, stood up, and danced, her long dress hanging crooked on her awkward, bulging body.

The Princess spun round, then held out her hand to invite the old minstrel to join her.

The minstrel did not respond.

The King stood and bellowed, "Why won't you take the hand of my daughter?"

The music stopped.

The minstrel bowed low, "I'm sorry, Sire, but I cannot see. I did not know she had offered her hand to me."

The King let go of all the anger he had stored up for so many years in a great, long laugh of relief.

The Princess took the hand of the minstrel and danced with him.

The minstrel stayed and played all through the day and into the night, joining the royal family for their evening meal.

"I must thank you," the King said after finishing his meal. "You provided a much-needed distraction."

"The pleasure was all mine, Sire. I have heard many a story of the good King of this land. And even more stories of the Princess who brings joy wherever she goes. Stories of generous gifts, of carrying heavy loads, of listening ears, and kind words."

"We love the people of our kingdom," the Princess said, blushing.

"Yes, we do," the King said in a contented tone.

The minstrel continued, "May I be so bold as to indulge in a curiosity?"

"Of course," the King boomed.

"Why would a King as generous and jolly as you and a Princess whose laugh brightens the very room around her need a distraction?"

The Princess burst out without thinking, "No one will marry me because I am too beautiful! The suitors come and are charmed for sure, but they won't take me for their bride because I am too beautiful."

"Is that so?" the minstrel questioned.

"I am afraid it is," said the King.

The minstrel stood and bowed low again. "If it is acceptable before the King, might I propose a solution?"

"It is more than acceptable. Out with it."

"It doesn't take eyes to see there are many young men within your own kingdom who are not afraid of your daughter's beauty. Perhaps a fitting suitor could be found here, closer to home."

"Why hadn't I thought of that?" the King sputtered. "Of course. It is true, there will never be a kingdom that loves you as much as our own." He looked at the Princess and said, "What do you think of this proposal?"

The Princess smiled and laughed, "It's perfect!"

And so it was that a long line of young men from their own kingdom came to court the Princess in hopes of winning her heart, for they knew a real beauty when they saw it.

THE DRAGON HATCHER

In the castle's long-forgotten west tower, a princess told a story to the only audience she could gather—a hard-boiled egg. It was a small, but quiet audience.

"Listen, and I will tell you my story," she said to the egg resting in her hand. "Once upon a time, there was a princess with seven beautiful sisters. Six older and one much younger. Her sisters frolicked through the castle in their pretty pastel gowns and did exactly as they pleased. But she did not. The seventh Princess spent most of her time alone in a tower . . . because she was ugly. I know you don't think princesses can be ugly, but this one was."

As she spoke, the egg began to grow. It expanded until it was the size and weight of one of the castle stones. The Princess placed the egg on her lap and watched as it changed color. An iridescent green swirled onto the egg's white canvas, covering it. The egg now resembled one of her mother's gem stones, sleek and shiny, but retained its egg shape.

"What kind of magic is this?" the Princess whispered.

She began her story again. "The Princess knew she would never be lovely like her sisters. She felt just like lacy undergarments, unnoticed and completely redundant. Nothing could be done about her big nose and splotchy skin, or her glasses. Princesses do not wear glasses." The Princess paused to see what would happen.

CRACK

The sound filled the cavernous room and echoed off the walls. A tiny claw appeared in the fissure of the egg. The Princess stifled a scream. Her heart was pounding so loud in her chest it seemed to echo in the room like a drum. She placed the egg on the floor and took refuge behind a large chair.

The egg rolled on the stone floor. More tiny claws appeared in the fissure and began to tear at the crevice until a small green snout emerged. The Princess's eyes moved between the egg and the door.

The top of the egg cracked and fell to the ground. There, in a heap of emerald shell, was a baby dragon.

The Princess was well acquainted with stories of dragons—their nasty dispositions and appetites for princesses—but . . . this dragon was different. So helpless. So small. So cute.

It was astonishing, really, how cute a baby dragon could be. With those big, round, playful eyes. And shiny green scales. Tiny wings. And that tail, spiked with tiny, purple stubs.

The dragon took a few unsteady steps and flitted its wings. The Princess grinned.

The dragon opened its mouth, revealing tiny, sharp, white teeth, then made a horrible screech. The Princess cowered behind the chair.

The dragon rolled around on its back, then turned on its round tummy and slithered across the floor. The Princess was about to run when the dragon saw her hiding. It hopped up and down on short, stumpy legs and waddled toward the Princess. When the dragon touched her velvet gown, it nuzzled her, and the Princess let go of the breath she had been holding.

"Oh, aren't you a sweet little dragon," the Princess cooed.

The dragon looked up and . . . was that a smile? The Princess was sure of it—the dragon smiled.

"Aren't you adorable? You wouldn't hurt anything, would you?" The Princess continued patting the dragon on the head. The dragon flapped its tiny wings and flopped down on its bottom. "No, you wouldn't hurt a thing. You can be my little dragon."

The Princess and the dragon played together in the tower all day. At nightfall, the Princess chose to sleep in the tower; she didn't want her little dragon to be afraid, or discovered.

The thick, woven rug did nothing to prevent the Princess from feeling the cold stone floor beneath her. Sleep came in short, restless spurts throughout the night.

Gradually, morning sunlight slipped through the window and slid down the wall, lighting the room.

When the light reached the Princess on the floor, she startled awake and saw the dragon hovering just above her face, staring down at her. She gulped, touched the dragon on its head, and said, "Hello, little friend. How are you this morning?" The dragon opened its mouth so wide the Princess rolled over and sat up abruptly. The close proximity of the dragon's teeth reminded her of their nasty reputations.

With mouth wide open, tongue extended and tight, the dragon let out a terrible, "SQUAWK!" The Princess covered her ears. The dragon flew in a short hop onto the Princess's lap. "SQUAWK!"

"What's wrong?"

"SQUAWK! SQUAWK! SQUAWK!" The sound filled the space like an un-tuned bell.

"What? What do you want?" the Princess asked, in desperation. The dragon snapped its jaws. "Oh, are you hungry?"

"SQUAWK!"

"Right. You stay here. I'll fetch some food from the dining hall."

The Princess straightened herself up, put on her most charming (and innocent) smile, and formulated a plan on her way to the dining hall. She burst in and said, "Mother, Father, I would like to take a large tray of food with me to the tower today to practice my still-life painting. Would that be all right?"

"Of course, darling. Let me call a servant to carry the tray for you."

"No, thank you. I can do it myself," she said sweetly, with a curtsy.

"All right, as you wish," her parents responded, already worn out from the conversation.

The Princess carried a tray, heavy with food, to the tower. Berries, mush, bread, cheese, honey, jam, hard-boiled eggs, chunks of ham, nuts, peaches, and a jug of milk were laid in front of the dragon. "I wasn't sure what you would like, so I brought a bit of everything." The Princess smiled at the dragon and patted it on the head. The dragon took a bite of each food offered, chewed thoughtfully, then spat each morsel onto the floor. The Princess grimaced at the mess and startled when . . .

"SQUAWK!" SQUAWK! SQUAWK!"

"I know you are hungry! But what do you eat?"

"SQUAWK! SQUAWK!"

"Shh, shh, listen, I'll tell you a story while I think."

The dragon hopped up onto the Princess's lap, its mouth quiet and curved into a smile. The Princess began, "Once upon a time, there was a princess who was ugly. So ugly she lived in a tower so she would not distress anyone with her appearance . . . " The Princess continued weaving the sad tale as she saw each thread in her mind. She felt the dragon, calm and heavy in her lap. Too heavy. She opened her eyes. The dragon had grown to twice its original size. "How odd," the Princess whispered.

The dragon hopped onto the floor and nipped at the Princess's dress with a playful look in its eye.

"You want to play?" the Princess smiled.

The dragon hopped, then tumbled on the floor. The Princess laughed, jumped up and ran around and around the dragon. The dragon sometimes tumbled, sometimes flitted in the air with its thin wings. The Princess twirled as if dancing with the dragon. The dragon hiccupped, and a tiny bit of flame escaped its mouth, igniting the Princess's dress. The Princess yelped in surprise and patted the fire out.

"Bad dragon!" she scolded. "Now you've gone and singed one of my best gowns!"

The dragon sat at her feet and closed its mouth. "That's right! Good dragon. We don't scorch princesses, do we?"

The dragon nodded.

"You are a good dragon. You are my friend."

That night, the Princess hid the dragon and asked her parents if she could move her bedroom to the west tower. She explained the view from the tower windows was ever so much better for painting landscapes.

Day after day, the Princess fed the dragon stories. It was not long before the Princess discovered it was not just any story the dragon wanted but *the* story; the story of the Princess who was so ugly, so hideous, she lived in a long-forgotten tower to spare her parents and the kingdom the fright of looking at her.

The dragon continued to double in size with each

telling, looking satisfied . . . and sinister. As the dragon continued to grow, there was less and less room for the Princess. The tower was filled up with the dragon's legs and arms and belly.

The dragon's breath made the room rather sweltering. The dragon's tail was always in the way: on her bed, in front of the door, blocking the window. The Princess constantly found herself asking, "Could you *please* move your tail?"

Most of her precious things were broken. Her mirror and armoire didn't last two weeks with the enormous dragon in such an awkward space. All her paintings were either smashed or scorched by the huge beast.

As uncomfortable as it was, the Princess spent all her time in the tower to keep her very large dragon a secret.

When the dragon was hungry, it stomped its feet, and the entire tower shook. Little bits of stone bounced free from the floor, filling the room with fine dust. The Princess ran to the dragon, placing her hands on its belly, and told the story to calm the beast. Each time, the dragon grew, even though there was no space in the tower left to fill.

One day, the Princess noticed her reflection in the dragon's shiny green scales. The curve of the scale made her nose look even larger, and her eyes looked small and dull. Her hair was singed at the edges, as was all of her clothing (another inconvenience of living with a dragon). Her cheeks looked thin, and the tint of green reflecting back at her brought tears to her eyes.

"I am even uglier than I was before. Absolutely hideous. No one will ever love me."

The dragon snarled, and flame burst from its mouth and out the tower window.

A knight in training saw the flame and ran for the castle gates. The flame came from the same tower where his favorite of the eight princesses was often seen painting at the window. The flame could only mean one thing: a dragon.

"There is a dragon in the west tower!" the Knight called out in alarm as he ran. "A dragon in the west tower! All are in great peril! Step aside!"

The Knight was given immediate entrance, ran up a good many steps, and tried to open the tower door. It wouldn't budge. The Knight rammed the door with his body over and over again, yelling, "I have come to save you, Princess!"

The Princess heard the Knight and thought, *Save me from what?*

The door began to bend, then break. It was only a matter of time before it buckled. The Princess did the only thing she could think to do; she hid in the curtains. *If he sees how ugly I am, he will run away.*

The door crashed to the floor, and the Knight tumbled in. With a quick roll, he was up on his feet, sword ready. He took one look at the dragon's enormous belly and ran forward, sword first, to dispatch this dragon.

The Princess watched from the curtains, feeling as

though she should stop the Knight from killing the dragon, but was too afraid to show herself.

The Knight's sword crumpled on impact. He held the sword in disbelief. The dragon let out a small burst of flame directly above the Knight, singeing him. He retreated for more weapons, cooler armor, and a better plan.

The Knight approached the throne room, armor still steaming, and explained to the King and Queen the dragon situation. "There is a dragon in the west tower. It is enormous and quite difficult to kill." He raised his sword as evidence. "I fear the seventh Princess is either dead or in great peril."

The Queen gasped. "How did a dragon get inside the tower in the first place? It seems we would have noticed something like that."

"I do not know, Your Majesty, but I recommend you address it immediately."

"Call for the royal knights! I want this dragon gone by morning," the King decreed.

Knights entered the tower through the door and windows, carrying ropes and chains to tie the dragon down and drag it out of the tower. The dragon roared and stomped. Bursts of flame caught hold of armor. Knight after knight left the tower uncomfortably hot. A group of knights working on securing the dragon's mouth with rope were tossed against the tower walls.

The Princess watched from behind the curtain as the dragon effortlessly defeated these brave men.

When the knights had all retreated, the dragon continued to stomp and roar, tail thrashing.

The Princess's body shook and tears ran down her face. She covered her ears in an effort to block out the dragon's loud, "SQUAWK! SQUAWK! SQUAWK!"

This dragon is powerful and frightening.

"SQUAWK! SQUAWK! SQUAWK!" The floor rumbled beneath the Princess's feet, and she could feel the temperature rise with each burst of the dragon's flame.

"Fine!" the Princess screamed from behind the curtain. "You'll have your story." In a trembling voice, the Princess whispered the story once again. The dragon lay its head by the curtain, eyes glowing like the embers of a fire, and once again, the dragon was calm.

The knights were sent by royal decree on a quest to find a way to kill the dragon. The tower was abandoned—although a few servants were assigned the daily task of delivering food in case the Princess was still alive.

One day, the Littlest Princess, the eighth daughter of the King and Queen, came twirling into the tower, pink cheeks glowing, dress spinning, so caught up in her play that she was completely unaware of any danger. She was singing, "I am a beautiful princess. A beautiful, beautiful princess."

The Princess was so surprised to see her little sister she jumped over the dragon's tail to meet her. She couldn't help but smile at the sweet scene before her. In the tiny bit of space unoccupied by the dragon, the Littlest Princess danced. For the first time since its arrival, the Princess temporarily forgot about the dragon. She twirled her sister around and around. "You are a beautiful princess!" They both laughed, filling the tower with this unfamiliar sound.

The Littlest Princess looked up at her sister and said, "You are a beautiful princess, too."

"No, I'm not." The words came out without her even thinking about them.

"You're not?"

"No, I am afraid not."

That's when the Littlest Princess noticed the dragon behind her sister and asked, "Where did that dragon come from?" The Littlest Princess's eyes were wide with surprise.

"I made it," the Princess answered with a flat tone.

"You did?"

"Yes," the Princess sighed.

"I want to make a dragon. Can you show me how?" The Littlest Princess glowed at the thought of making her very own dragon.

"No!" The Princess replied a little too sharply. "You do not want a dragon like this."

"Why not? Will it eat me?"

"It might."

"But it hasn't eaten you."

"No, but it might. And with a dragon this size, who is always hungry, there is just no space to really live anymore."

The Littlest Princess pouted and stomped her feet. "But I want a dragon. I want to be just like you!"

"No, you don't!" The Princess shook with emotion, and the Littlest Princess left the tower crying.

The dragon licked the Princess. Its soft, leathery tongue felt like a snake crawling up her back. The Princess shuddered and ran to the corner where she could hide among the broken furniture.

I do not want this dragon anymore, but what can I do?

The dragon, SQUAWKED! and started stomping and thrashing about.

The Princess cowered in the corner, shaking. She stared at the door. *It has been a long time since I've left the tower.* She grabbed the frame of her broken mirror and stood to face the dragon. With fury in her eyes, the Princess said, "Hungry? Well, you are going to have to go to bed without your supper tonight!"

The dragon snapped at the Princess, snagging her dress with its teeth and pulled her closer. The Princess struggled free and ran out the door. The air smelled different, fresher, outside the tower.

The dragon roared and stomped, then flames poured out of the tower, but the Princess did not go back. Instead, she looked for something to slay her dragon with.

She found a bow and arrow in the armory and rat poison in the kitchen. A plan began to formulate in her mind. *Perhaps if I shot a poison dipped arrow into the mouth of the dragon, the poison would do its work from the inside out, and the dragon would die.*

The Princess practiced with the bow until she felt she had mastered it enough to hit her rather large (and loud) target. She ran back to the tower and kicked open the door. The dragon looked at her and opened its mouth with a, "SQUAWK!"

The Princess shot the arrow and watched as it sailed deep into the dragon's throat. The dragon coughed and hissed, then swallowed the arrow. The Princess watched, eyes wide, to see what would happen next.

Nothing. Absolutely nothing. The dragon continued to bellow, thrashing so hard against the walls of the tower that chunks of the ceiling fell, opening the tower to the starry night sky.

"What am I supposed to do?" the Princess yelled up at the stars.

Then, a curious thing happened; one of the stars streaked down from the sky and flew through the window.

A tiny fairy, glowing silver, hovered right beside her. With a quick flick of her wand, the fairy stilled and silenced the dragon.

"Who—who are you?" the Princess stammered.

"I am your fairy godmother."

"Really?" The Princess looked at the tiny fairy in disbelief.

"Really." The fairy smiled.

"I wish for you to make this dragon go away."

"I cannot do that."

"Why not?" The Princess stomped her foot in frustration. "You obviously have the power to take care of this dragon." She pointed, arm shaking, at the still and silent beast. "Why won't you make it go away?

The fairy's eyes twinkled above her soft cheeks as she smiled at the Princess.

The Princess's cheeks flushed. "What kind of fairy godmother are you, anyway?"

"The kind that loves you enough to let you fix this problem on your own."

"I can't!" The Princess burst into sloppy, snotty tears. "This dragon can't be killed. Brave men have tried. I have tried, but this dragon is impossible to kill!"

"To kill? Yes, quite impossible. To change, no."

"What?"

"You created the beast, my dear; you can change it."

"How?"

But the fairy burst into a bright, silver light and was gone. The dragon was free from the fairy's spell and resumed its thrashing and shrieking.

"Seriously?!" the Princess screamed into the sky. She felt like crumpling to the floor and letting the dragon eat her, but instead, she screamed at the dragon. "Enough!" The dragon continued to rage.

"Stop!" the Princess yelled with all her might.

The dragon did not respond.

"I will not feed you any longer, you horrible beast!"

The dragon blew out so much fire she could barely

breathe. But the Princess was filled with fury. "I will not let you control my life any longer! I am a princess!"

The dragon stopped and stared at the Princess. Fear shone in its amber eyes.

The Princess swallowed her fear and sputtered, "You want a story?! Try this one: I am a beautiful princess, and this tower is no longer my home." The words of this story felt like a question and came out with false bravado, but they came. "I am a beautiful and powerful princess who created a dragon. The dragon grew so enormous and fierce and threatening that the Princess forgot she was the one who created it. Then, one day, she understood. She understood she could also change the dragon with her story."

The dragon roared in pain and blew flames into the sky.

The Princess continued to whisper the story into the room. "I am a beautiful and powerful princess who can change a dragon with a story."

The quiet words of this story filled the space. The dragon slumped to the ground and a small burst of flame escaped its mouth. The Princess smiled and continued. This story seemed to deplete the dragon's energy.

A glint of green caught the Princess's eye, and she watched as a few of the dragon's impenetrable scales came loose and fell from its body. As the scales tumbled to the ground, their luminescence reflected and threw light around the room. Just before they clinked on the ground, the scales folded in half. When they opened up again, they were no longer hard and shiny, but soft and light. They were flittering. The scales took flight as dainty butterflies. Gorgeous and green, the butterflies fluttered out the window and into the big blue sky.

Each day, the Princess's story sounded less like a question. "I am a beautiful and powerful princess who can change a dragon with a story."

The dragon's body was still. Its squawk squelched.

Over time and telling, the Princess believed this story to be true. "I am a beautiful and powerful princess who can change a dragon with *my* story."

And so it was, that the once fierce and un-slayable dragon flitted out the window as thousands of beautiful butterflies.

DISCOVERING THE REAL BEAUTY IN YOU

A Discussion Guide

When you seek beauty in all people and all things, you will not only find it; you will become it.

— *Unknown*

THE RAVENOUS GOWN

*A real princess is so much more than a
beautiful ball gown.*

—*Steffani Raff*

Questions

What could you miss if you only engage in conversation
and/or friendship with those people who are physically
attractive at first sight?

What have you observed about the way you or others
treat another person based on their clothing and/or phys-
ical appearance?

Just for Fun

When I was in my early twenties, I did an experiment.
I went shopping at the mall, looking my worst. I wore
worn-out clothes, no make-up, glasses, and pulled my
hair back in a messy braid. A week later, I went back to
the mall, this time paying special attention to my appearance. I wore my best outfit, made sure my make-up and
hair were just right, and put in my contacts.

I wanted to see if my appearance changed the way
people treated me. The difference was stunning. I went
mostly unnoticed by salespeople the first time. I was rarely approached, and when I was, they did not try to engage

me in conversation or help me find what I was looking for. When I went back, looking fabulous, salespeople approached me, asked me more questions about what I was looking for, and went out of their way to help me find it.

I hadn't changed—but my appearance had.

Story Note

The seed this story grew from was a Middle Eastern folktale. In this culture, there are many stories of a wise fool named Hodja. In one story, he comes to a banquet dressed in his work clothes and is thrown out. When he comes back in a fine coat and trousers, he is offered the place of honor. In what seems a rather foolish gesture, he feeds his coat, then shares the wisdom of not judging a person by their clothing.

This has long been a favorite story of mine, and I wondered how the message would come across if the main character was a princess instead of an old man. The images that came to my mind while creating this story both surprised and delighted me; I hope they did for you, too.

THE MAGIC MIRROR

Happiness is our most attractive accessory.

—Unknown

Questions

Why do you think the shepherdess in this story had the courage to look into the King's mirror? Why didn't any of the other women in the kingdom look?

When the shepherdess finally approaches the mirror, the other women are quick to point out her flaws. Why do you think that is? What kind of damage might occur when you choose to focus on the flaws of either yourself or others?

I've heard it said that genetics gives you the face of your youth, but when you are eighty, you get the face you deserve. What kind of face would you like to have when you are eighty years old? How do you think you can get it?

Story Note

The structure of this story came from a folktale from Spain. I re-imagined it to create this new version.

CINDERELLA—SORT OF

If the shoe doesn't fit; break it.

—*Steffani Raff*

Questions

How do you think age changes your idea of "happily ever after"?

What is the "shoe" or *ideal* of our day? What does the promise of "happily ever after" look like today if we can just fit the "shoe"?

The heroine in this story cuts off part of her foot in order to fit the shoe. Are there extreme measures that girls/women feel they need to take to fit the ideal of our society today? Do you think these measures are necessary and desirable? Why or why not?

Just for Fun

Watch this one-minute movie Dove put together called "Evolution."

What does it tell you about our society's *shoe* or *ideal*? What is the danger of trying to fit this shoe?

THE LOST PRINCESS

*Whatever you believe about yourself on the
inside is what will be visible on the outside.*

—*Unknown*

Questions

Do you think the story we tell ourselves is so powerful
that it can actually change the way we look? Or act? What
stories do you tell yourself? Are they true, or just the only
story you know?

When Princess Ronwynn finally fights against the story she has been told her whole life, she says, "I am not a dirty rat! I am not a stupid fish. I am not a pig." But these statements do not have the power to change her. When she finally tells herself the story, "I am a princess. My father is a king. My mother a queen," it changes her. Are there ways you define yourself by what you are not? What might happen if you replaced that definition with something you *are*?

What good things occur because of the curse? Does Princess Ronwynn view what happened to her as a curse or a gift? Has there ever been a hard thing you experienced that ended up being a gift?

A REAL PRINCESS

We like someone because. We love someone although.

—Henri De Montherlant

Questions

Is it natural to fret about your flaws and try to hide them? What happens to the Princess when she reveals her *stinky* flaw? What do you think could happen to you if you reject the idea of having to be perfect?

How do you think you find a "prince" who will love you through Ever-After, happily?

What qualities do you need to develop and practice to really love another person?

Just for Fun

I created this story as a bedtime story for my daughter one night. She wanted a story about a princess, and I wanted her to grow up believing a princess is more than a ball gown. (And at the time, she had really stinky feet.)

THE PRINCESS WHO COULD FLY

*The meaning of life is to find your gift. The
purpose of life is to give it away.*

—William Shakespeare

Questions

After seeking her gift for some time, the Princess discovers she can fly. Do you believe each person has a unique gift? What can you learn about discovering your own gifts through the story?

The people in the kingdom think the Princess is extraordinary, why?

How do you think the Princess knew what to show people when she took them flying? How did it help them? Has anyone ever showed you a solution to your problem by helping you see something differently, without telling you what to do? How did that work for you?

THE STORY TREE

The best and most beautiful things in the world cannot be seen or even touched. They must be felt with the heart.

—*Helen Keller*

Questions

How did knowing the old woman's stories help the children accept her differences? How can you learn to look past the differences you see in others (e.g., age, social status, religion, race, appearance, and education level)?

What are some good ways to learn a person's story?

Why is the old woman surprised when the girl says, "You're not a tree—you're a grandmother"? How does the woman's self-perception prevent her from viewing herself as others see her? Do you have any experiences where your self-perception blocked you from seeing what others saw in you?

Do you have any experiences about someone you learned to see differently because you were able to learn their story?

MOONSTONES
AND MAGIC

*People are like stained-glass windows. They
sparkle and shine when the sun is out, but
when darkness sets in, their true beauty is
revealed only if there is a light from within.*

—Elizabeth Kubler-Ross

Questions

What character qualities create the light that shines in
Catherine when she experiences darkness? Are there other qualities not mentioned in the story that you feel create
light inside a person?

What is the role of adversity in our lives? Do you think
having the courage to do hard things can make a person
more beautiful? Have you seen any examples of this in
your own life, or in the lives of other people you know?

Just for Fun

My grandpa was a geologist and found a moonstone while
working in India. My grandma later had this moonstone
made into a necklace for me. I love the necklace because it
reminds me of them, and I wear it often. There is a legend
about putting a moonstone under your tongue during a
full moon so you can see the future. And yes, I tried it!

Story Note

The bones for this story came from Andrew Lang's prolific collection of Fairy Stories. I took the structure and re-imagined it to create this story. The quote about people being like stained glass windows mentioned above, inspired me and wove itself into the images I used to tell this story.

THE CRYSTAL CASTLE

You are no better or worse than anyone else.

—*Anonymous*

Questions

In what ways can the Prince's nose be a metaphor for individual weaknesses or flaws?

What happens to the Prince's self-perception when his parents celebrate this *flaw* as something that indicates his superiority?

When the Prince acknowledges his *flaw*, the crystal walls that stop him from connecting with the Princess he loves disappear. How does acknowledging our own weaknesses give us power to love and connect with someone else more perfectly?

Story Note

The beginnings of this story came from a folktale I read long ago. As always, I re-invent these stories in my mind, and they often don't look a thing like the original tales they started from.

THE HEALING STONE

A man sees in the world what he carries in his heart.

—Faust, *by Johan Wolfgang von Goethe*

Questions

How does Sophie's ability to believe in something she cannot see change her village? How does it change her? Do you have any similar experiences?

In the story, there were voices with the power to build and encourage, and other voices with the power to tear down and discourage. Sometimes there are only subtle differences between them. How do you come to recognize which voices are which in your own life? What did Sophie's simple solution to the negative voices show you about handling voices unworthy of your attention?

How did you imagine Sophie's appearance? Nothing was said in the story about what she looked like. Why do you think you imagined her appearance the way you did?

Story Note

The idea for the voices in the stone came from an old Arabian folktale. The rest of the story I imagined, but I was later surprised and delighted to discover a Swiss legend that included a dragon, a healing stone, and moon milk.

THE CRANE'S GIFT

The most beautiful act of faith is the one made in darkness, in sacrifice, and with extreme effort.

—St. Pio of Pietreleina

Questions

How does discovering the woman's transformation and sacrifice change the husband's perception of his wife?

Do you believe the woman exhibited strength or weakness in her gentle, self-sacrificing gift to her husband? Discuss the reasoning behind your answer.

What changes occur to a woman's body over her lifetime? What can you learn about the perception of these changes, for both men and women, through this metaphorical story?

Story Note

The origin of this story comes from a Japanese folktale.

FETCH ME A STAR

Beauty may only be skin deep, but ugly goes clear to the bone.

—*Redd Foxx*

Questions

Did you think the Princess in this story was beautiful? How did the way she treated others change your impression of her beauty?

Have you ever had an experience where something you thought you really wanted, but didn't get, turned out to be a good thing? Tell the story of that discovery.

Story Note

The seed for this story came from an English folktale. I have always loved the riddle in the story and played with the idea of changing the main character from the original story into a knight who was on a quest for true love. Once I did that, all kinds of funny scenes emerged in my mind involving this sweet, awkward knight.

THE RELUCTANT KNIGHT

No one can make you feel inferior without your consent.

—Eleanor Roosevelt

Questions

The Princess didn't feel like she was perceived as brave or smart because she was a girl. Do you think these perceptions exist today? If so, what do you think can be done to change them?

The Princess in this story didn't feel like she would be taken seriously unless she was in a man's role. Have you ever felt this way? Describe your experience.

What happened when the Princess chose to embrace her femininity instead of choosing to become a knight?

BEAUTY'S CURSE

It is not what you look at that matters. It's what you see.

—Henry David Thoreau

Questions

How does the King in this story protect, honor, and pre-serve his daughter's own unique beauty? What power do parents have in a girl's developing perception of what she looks like?

How is the Princess in this story beautiful? What do you think makes a person beautiful?

Just for Fun

My oldest son was born with disabilities. There have been many times when children have responded to the differences in his appearance, speech, and intellect by making fun of him or by ignoring him. Listen to this story about an experience we had when children learned to see my son for who he really is. Have you had a similar experience you can share? Is there anyone in your life you could offer friendship to?

Story Note

The beginnings of this story came from a Romanic folk-tale. The more I thought about this unique princess, the more the story evolved into what it is now.

CPSIA information can be obtained
at www.ICGtesting.com
Printed in the USA
FSOW01n1938120215
5150FS

9 781939 629593